The Case of the Grease Monkey's Uncle.

JOE WELLS

ISBN: 978-1-9160-2912-5

DEDICATION

To my wife Angella, for her patience having to listen to me shouting at my computer when trying to upload this book!

CONTENTS

ACKNOWLEDGMENTS

World War Two, the forties, the Bentley Drivers Club and all my friends in the forties scene who helped inspire this book.

THE BEGINNING.

The opening of any new business endeavour is often fraught with chaos and confusion and so it was with the opening of the detective agency of James Arbuttnott and Archibald Cluff on the 21st January 1947 when they attempted to move into their new premises.

James was the taller of the two, with wavy fair hair and a moustache to match, very much the Officer and Gentleman and although of Scottish descent he had no trace of an accent, educated at Eton he had that distinguished confident air that immediately says, good breeding whilst his colleague was shorter and an altogether rougher diamond with ginger hair, from the East End of London, it would be true to say that one was tall and good looking whilst the other was not so lucky in the looks department and was built like a brick out house.

Their new office was above a lady's dress and lingerie emporium called Madame Fifi which gave the impression the owner may have been of French extraction, but was in fact owned by a middle-aged lady called Ethel Burrows who was once lady's maid to Lady Georgina Appleby before opening her shop.

They arrived early that morning and James parked his 4½ Bentley in the road opposite Madame Fifi at 50 Chiltern Street W1 and while glancing up at the office above he said. "Well Archie we're finally here at last, now we can really get moving."

As they crossed the road Ethel Burrows who was quite petite and looked somewhat younger than her 41 years of age was in the window of her shop placing some rather fancy French knickers in the window display and on seeing the two men she waved and mouthed "good luck." They waved back and entered the door which was to the right of her window which led up to their office and on passing James took his handkerchief from his top pocket and gave the brass plaque which said Arbuthnott and Cluff Detective Agency a quick polish.

Halfway up the stairs they were met with the aroma of new wood and beeswax polish when a voice called out, "guv'nor, we've got your furniture on the van do you want us to bring it up?"

James stopped and turned. "Yes, please just bring it up the stairs thank you, but please be very careful of the wood panelling on the walls, we've only just had them done." The office itself was panelled in wood veneer, interspersed with panels made from a mix of brass, copper and aluminium based on a design he'd seen on the RMS Queen Mary liner before the war, together with stunning half-moon iridescent green glass wall lights and looked extremely stylish.

They had ordered some rather impressive Art Deco desks and chairs, complete with desk lamps and matching filing cabinets and all the trimmings. "So much better than all that Utility rubbish we had in the war," thought James who was a man who appreciated quality in everything.

"Where do you want 'em guv'nor?" said the delivery man who was rather small but seemed to be the foreman, who together with his assistant a considerably larger somewhat rotund man, proceeded to hump all three desks and assorted paraphernalia up the flight of stairs that led to the offices.

The larger man was now puffing like a steam train and growing ever redder in the face as time passed. "Pardon me sir, but I wonder if I could have a glass of water," he said as he collapsed into one of the desk chairs.

"Yes of course old chap," said James. "Archie, fetch this poor fellow a glass of water will you please?"

Archie dashed out of the office and came back with a rather splendid cut glass Champagne flute.

“Pushing the boat out there, aren’t we Archie?”

“They’re all I could find, I haven’t had time to unpack yet,” said Archie, as he passed the glass to the wheezing delivery man.

Taking the glass, he said. “Shame it’s not full of bubbly sir, I quite like a glass of bubbly whenever I can get it.”

“I’m afraid you’re out of luck here chum,” said Archie laughing.

In the meantime, James and the foreman had been shifting the desks about in an attempt to find the perfect placing for them in the office and eventually the wheezing delivery man was sufficiently recovered to stand up and leave.

“Lovely desks guv’nor, you can’t beat a bit of walnut,” said the delivery foreman, “need them moved again, or are we happy, Sir?”

“No thank you, we’re happy where they are now,” said James, who was by now lounging in his desk chair dreaming of clients to come.

Jumping up quickly he discreetly placed half a crown in the foreman’s hand and led him to the door and saw him out.

“Well Archie, all we need now is a phone and a secretary,” and with that there was a knock on the door.

"GPO sir," said the voice from the other side of the door, a voice which somehow didn't seem to fit with the rather dapper fellow, who complete with pencil moustache and Macassar oiled black hair entered the office.

"Come to fix your phone Sir," he said. "I've got two desk phones a switchboard and enough cable to reach to Trafalgar Square, I may be some time!"

"Come in, come in you'd better get a move on I've got secretaries to interview and by the look of it here's one now," said James.

"Morning sir, my name's Doreen, may I come in?"

A rather timid looking young girl wearing spectacles stood in the doorway and James gestured for her to enter.

"Yes, indeed Doreen do come in," said James, "do mind the cable we don't want a nasty accident just take the seat in front of the desk and I'll pop round the other side."

"Now, how's your shorthand?"

"Not good Sir, I'm a bit of a beginner."

"And your speed typing, what speed can you type at?"

"Well sir, I'm a bit slow to tell the truth, I'm a bit of a beginner."

"How about switchboard experience?" James paused, "don't tell me, you're a bit of a beginner!"

"Well thank you for coming Doreen, just leave your address with my partner Archie and we'll be in touch in a day or so."

"See the young lady out will you Archie?"

Archie opened the door for Doreen who went out, passing a stunning young lady with blonde hair coming up the stairs, she had a fabulous hourglass figure and looked more suitable for an audition at The Palladium Theatre than the position currently offered by James and Archie.

She strutted into the office as if taking part in a Paris fashion show, sat in the chair, crossed her legs and produced a cigarette holder complete with cigarette and placed it between her ruby red lips.

"Mind if I smoke?" she said. "My name's Amelia Cruickshank and I'm delighted to meet you; do you have anything you'd like to ask me?"

"I certainly have," spluttered Archie.

"Thank you, Archie," said James. "I think I can handle the interview from here, do please smoke, I think I may join you it's been a rather stressful morning, a gasper should be just the job."

He took a cigarette from the box on his desk and lit it

and the one in Miss Cruickshank's holder. "Now, Miss Cruickshank," he paused.

"Miss Cruickshank, you're a very attractive looking young woman if you don't mind me saying so but this job entails more than looks, although I'm sure all the male clients would be only too happy to be entertained by you whilst they are waiting but we do need competence with typing and shorthand too."

"Oh Sir, you are a card, what on earth gave you the idea I wasn't suitable for the job, I can manage 90 words a minute for typing and 120 shorthand and I'm fully trained on the very latest GPO switchboard equipment, you'll have no trouble with my ability to do the job Sir."

"Right," said James. "Well you seem more than ideally suited for the job when would you like to start?"

"Would now do," she said, "I can make tea for a start, then I can have a look at your filing system," and with that she strutted off into the other room to make tea.

"She's a bit of a cracker," said the GPO man.

"She certainly is," said James. "I think we've struck lucky here, beauty and brains, what more can we ask?"

A disjointed voice was heard from the room next door. "I forgot to mention I'm fully competent in Morse code too!"

"Why am I not surprised by that," said Archie.

Sometime later Miss Cruickshank came back into the office carrying a tray of tea cups and a plate of biscuits.

“You can’t beat a good cuppa,” she said, “white with one sugar for you Mr Arbuthnott and two without for Mr Cluff and Mr GPO.”

“How did you know I took sugar,” asked James.

“Miss Cruickshank thought for a moment and said, “to tell the truth sir, I don’t know I’ve just got a way of knowing sometimes, I had a distant cousin who was a fortune teller, perhaps I get it from her.”

“I knew you were going to say that,” said the GPO man laughing.

“And your name is George Smith,” parried Miss Cruickshank.

“Good God, how on earth did you know that,” asked George.

“Simple,” she replied, “I saw the paperwork in your bag!”

They both laughed.

“You’ve only been here a matter of a little while but you continue to impress Miss Cruickshank,” said James. “I was under the impression that biscuits were still rationed, how on earth did you manage that?”

"Oh, I've got my ways Sir!" She said.

Having drunk his tea and wolfed down two digestive biscuits George the GPO man started to pack his bag to leave.

"Good Lord, that was quick," said Archie. "Are you sure it's working properly?"

"Oh yes sir, I'm positive I've been doing this so long now I could do it in the dark with one hand tied behind my back."

Archie's mind was racing ahead, "So you know everything there is to know about telephones do you George?"

"Well Mr Archie Sir, I'm not one for boasting but what I don't know about telephones isn't worth knowing, if I say so myself."

"So, George and this is just a hypothetical question, if I were to ask if it was possible for you to eavesdrop someone else's telephone conversation would you be able to assist me in that regard, hypothetically you understand?"

George smiled, "I can do that hypothetically, yes Sir."

"And what if I asked you to do it in real life?"

"Hypothetically or real life it's all the same to me sir, I'm never averse to earning a few shillings, my wife Mary is partial to the odd port and lemon and they're not cheap nowadays, I'm assuming this would be a cash job Sir, obviously we wouldn't want the GPO involved they have tendency not to look too kindly on employees moonlighting you understand."

"Oh yes George this would be cash and very hush hush you might say."

"Sounds good to me Sir, I'll give you my phone number and you can contact me when you need me."

Archie looked surprised, "you have a telephone George?"

"Of course, I have a phone Sir, perks of the job, if you get my drift."

"Yes, George I certainly do get your drift."

"Well goodbye Sir, Mr James, Miss Cruickshank," said George, "there's just one more thing, I was wondering if that last digestive is going begging?"

"It is indeed George, you enjoy it," said Miss Cruickshank.

"Oh, it's not for me Miss, it's a little gift for my wife Mary, she's partial to a digestive biscuit Sir."

With that he took the biscuit, gave his phone number to Miss Cruickshank, said goodbye again and departed down the stairs to the street, whistling the popular Max

Miller tune, "I fell in love with Mary from the dairy."

Miss Cruickshank stood up, "Time for tea sir?"

"It certainly is Miss Cruickshank, it certainly is," agreed James who took the opportunity to have a wander around the room.

The office was laid out in such a way that when entering from the street door and arriving at the top of the stairs one would be met by Miss Cruickshank in her portioned off part of the office where one might wait before being escorted through to the main office to be greeted by James and Archie.

As he passed the desks, he ran his hand over the splendid burr walnut and stood back to admire the two semi-circular desks set at right angles to each other, with two matching semi-circular chairs placed in front of each and was very pleased with the overall look of the office.

He moved closer to the window and gazed down into the street to see his 4½ litre Bentley parked across the road and thought back to his time during the war and remembered his work for SOE which was based only two streets away at 64 Baker Street. "Interesting times," he thought.

It wasn't long before Miss Cruickshank came back into the office with more tea, "you can't beat a good cuppa," she said as she sat in one of the chairs in front of

James's desk.

"As you say Miss Cruickshank, you can't beat a good cuppa," said James as he looked her up and down. "So do please tell us about yourself my dear, I have to say you seem quite an intriguing character."

"Me Sir, no Sir there's very little to tell, truth be told."

"I was born in Shropshire in a very sleepy little village called Donnington, my father was a Vicar and my mother was a housewife, really quite dull."

"Father was quite a strict disciplinarian in many ways so I had to excel at school work which I did although it wasn't that difficult for me as I have an almost photographic memory which obviously helped, I'm fluent in French and German and oddly I have a smattering of Serbo Croate which I picked up from one of my tutors who came from the Balkans."

"You never cease to amaze us Miss Cruickshank," said James, "do please continue."

"I enjoyed school in many ways especially the art classes which I think I got from my mother who was quite a distinguished amateur artist, she actually had a couple of her paintings exhibited in the Royal Academy summer exhibition and of course I loved the Greek dancing which we did on the school lawn, it was a time when I could rebel a little from my rather stiff and rather restricting upbringing and let my emotions go."

Archie smiled as he imagined Miss Cruickshank dancing on her school lawn whilst letting her emotions go during school Greek dancing class wearing nothing more than a flimsy diaphanous flowing gown, "quite a sight," he thought to himself.

"I did my School Certificate which I passed in all six subjects including Maths and English and passed with distinction but I didn't stay on to do the Higher School Certificate, by that time I was getting a little bored with scholarly endeavour and was looking for something a little more creative, I finally left home at eighteen searching for adventure, needless to say father was not impressed."

"The day I left father wished me well and I knew he'd forgiven me for leaving, he was a Vicar after all but mother gave me a little kiss on the cheek and I could tell from the look in her eye she would have loved to have done the same when she was younger, but that was different times and it would have been unthinkable then."

"So, you became a secretary?" questioned Archie.

"Oh no sir, I became what you might call an exotic dancer."

"Blimey," said Archie slightly perplexed.

"It all started when I met a friend of mine for a drink and he brought his girlfriend with him and we were chatting and I mentioned how much I enjoyed dancing when I was at school and she mentioned she was working as a dancer just round the corner in Great Windmill Street and I should come for an audition and that's how I found myself outside The Windmill Theatre the next day."

"To say I was terrified would be an understatement but Mrs Henderson was very pleasant and it's amazing what a rush of adrenaline can do, I must say I was extremely naïve I hadn't thought of dressing for the audition I'd just gone in twin set and pearls."

"You can't dance like that ducky," she said, "take your skirt and slip off we're all girls together here, well except for Jimmy on the piano and he's a Nancy boy anyway."

"As I said Sir, I was a tad naïve and it wasn't until sometime later when I found out what a Nancy boy actually was."

"Well I thought, I'm here auditioning on the stage of The Windmill Theatre, what have I got to lose so I whipped off my skirt and slip and got on with it, I kept my pearls on though I still wanted to look like a lady."

"Ruby the dance captain took the audition and I'm glad to say the routine was much easier than I was expecting and when we'd finished Mrs Henderson called from the darkness of the stalls, I want number one, number three and number seven, well done girls, here tomorrow at ten for rehearsals and that was it, I was in!"

"The next day at rehearsals was I in for a surprise, we spent all morning learning the routine then broke for lunch and back to clean the dance in the afternoon."

"Imagine my surprise when Ruby said, alright girls we'll have a full run through after tea including the tableaux vivant, well I had no idea what she was on about so I asked one of the other girls who laughed and said nudes dear, nudes."

"Right in the middle of our dance routine was placed a naked girl shielded with large fans, I had no idea as she had been clothed all during the rehearsals and at the end of the dance she moved the fans and there she stood motionless in the altogether, apparently it wasn't against the law as long as she didn't move." "Well I thought, so this is showbusiness!"

"I'd been having a gay old time for almost a year and then that fateful day on the 3rd of September 1939 when we all gathered around the wireless to hear Mr Chamberlain's speech, I can remember it even now."

Miss Cruickshank put on a silly voice as if to impersonate Neville Chamberlain, "This morning the British ambassador in Berlin handed the German government a final note stating that unless we heard from them by 11 o'clock that they were prepared at once to withdraw their troops from Poland, a state of war would exist between us. I have to tell you now that no such undertaking has been received, and that consequently this country is at war with Germany."

"Well I thought, if it's war I could be dead tomorrow and Mrs Henderson had been asking me for ages if I'd like to have a go at the tableaux, you've got a cracking body, she said and I thought, well I've nothing to lose so I told her I'd give it a try and that's how I became one of the famous Windmill nudes!"

"The night I went on for my first tableaux Mr Van Damm the manager of the theatre, who was also known as V.D. came and reminded me, we can only get away with this because we have convinced the Lord Chamberlain that nudity in theatres was not obscene or every nude statue in every museum would be illegal." "Never forget," he said, "If you move, it's rude!"

"Very popular was the tableaux, so much so that when one ended and the audience left those chaps at the back of the theatre would bound over the empty seats to sit at the front for the next tableaux, we all called it the Windmill steeplechase."

"It was actually V.D. who helped me get my next proper break in the business, he heard me singing in the dressing room one day and said, with a voice like that I should be auditioning for E.N.S.A and I said, what's that?" "Well it turns out it was a new organisation formed by Leslie Hanson and Basil Dean who were actors and film producers."

"If you remember I mentioned Jimmy who played the piano when I first auditioned for The Windmill, well by now I'd found out what a Nancy boy was and he'd become one of my best friends, anyway his boyfriend used to do arrangements for the band so together they sorted a couple of songs for me and away I went."

"There were so many people at the audition, some extremely good and some really quite average which made me think I might be in with a chance, I gave it my best shot and got the usual response when I left, don't call us we'll call you, so I left the number of the Stage Door at the Windmill where they could contact me and came back to my digs feeling a little dejected."

"The girls saw I was a little low and said don't worry dear you never know and we opened a bottle of whiskey which one of them produced from nowhere, Lord knows where she got it from and nobody asked and we had a good old sing song together which perked me up no end."

"About a week later I was coming into the theatre for an afternoon matinee when Tom the doorman said a Mr Dean had called for me and I was to call him back as soon as I could, which I did straight away thinking it was going to be one of those, thanks for coming but no thanks calls." "Blimey, was I surprised, they wanted me, they actually wanted me, I mean I'd never thought of myself as a singer it was just something I did for fun, singing for the girls with Jimmy on the piano, you could have knocked me down with a feather!"

"That night after our show, myself and some of the girls got together with some Army chaps they knew who were on leave, it had only been four months ago since they escaped from the beaches of Dunkirk in 1940 when the Nazis pushed the whole Army back to the sea, they must have had an awful time poor devils, so we were cheering them up and celebrating my leaving to join E.N.S.A at the same time."

"This was now September 1940 and the Blitz had started, it went on every night for eight months, the ruddy Germans bombing London but this was only the start but we were not going to let a few bombs spoil our fun, in fact we had a moto at the Windmill, We Never Close and we didn't right through the war."

"We went to The Café de Paris which wasn't too far down the road which had two advantages, firstly it wasn't too far away in Coventry Street which helped in finding our way in the black out and it was also below ground which made us think we'd be safe from the bombs." "Mind you, if a bomb had your name on it you were a goner, I used to admire everyone walking through the bomb-damaged streets to go to work the morning after a big raid, we weren't going to be beaten."

"Yes, I remember it being downstairs, the staircase went either side of the stage from the upper level I seem to remember, I used to go there before the war," said James, remembering safer times, "we didn't have so much time for that sort of thing later on."

"All of us drank and danced the night away, the band was superb and the girls said, not long before you'll be performing here and I thought, yes I will, I really will." "For some strange reason I was drawn to one of the boys, his name was Norman and he was badly shaken up from his experience on the beach in Dunkirk, I felt so sorry for him, I kept seeing this picture of him lying face down in the sand with blood coming from his ear, as I said Sir, sometimes I just know." "He was later killed in the desert of North Africa; I had the right image but the wrong sand."

"To say I was thrown in at the deep end is a bit of an understatement, singing with a full-blown band is an enormous challenge compared to singing for the girls with Jimmy on piano but I rose to the challenge and was soon performing all over London." "We played some fabulous gigs in some of the most stunning buildings in London although always a favourite were those in a basement away from the bombs, Quaglino's was absolutely gorgeous, as was The Dorchester which was built by Sir Robert McAlpine who was affectionately known as Concrete Bob as the building was made of concrete although it had stunning Art Deco interiors and seemed as safe as houses."

"Ironic that we thought the basement gigs were the

safest for on the 8th March 1941, a night I will never forget as long as I live, we were playing the Café de Paris which was a basement and we thought was literally as safe as houses." "I was booked to perform with Ken Snakehips Johnson and his band, I was in the dressing room and I could hear the introduction on the tannoy and I thought, I've time for a quick pee as I'm not on until after the opening number so I quickly popped to the loo." "The next thing I remember was waking up still sitting on the loo covered in dust and debris with an ARP Warden who suggested I might like to pull my draws up before they carried me out." "I came out at the same time as a chap on a stretcher who turned to the crowd and commented that at least he didn't have to pay for his meal which caused a cheer."

"Tragically Snakehips was killed along with his saxophonist Baba Williams and I lost my friend Jimmy and his boyfriend which was very sad as they shouldn't have been there that night but were depping for another couple of musicians who couldn't make the gig, we found out later that two bombs had somehow fallen down the ventilation shaft, what's the odds on that, Sir?"

"War isn't fair, is it Miss Cruickshank?" said Archie.

"No Sir, it isn't," she replied.

"I became a regular with Henry Hall and his band, if I had a pound for every factory or NAFFI I've performed in I'd be a lot better off than I am today," giggled Miss Cruickshank.

"I don't know if you gentlemen remember Henry Hall always used to close with Here's to the Next Time and do you remember Teddy Bears Picnic," asked Miss Cruickshank.

"Yes," said James, "I remember him on the wireless before the war," and went on to do a very bad impersonation of the man. "This is Henry Hall speaking."

"Yes Sir, that's the man, even with your rather bad impersonation I can see it as if it's yesterday."

"You were very busy in the war Miss Cruickshank, do tell us more," said James.

"There's not much more to tell Sir, I was recruited towards the end of the war to Stars in Battledress and went to North Africa, briefly performing with Nat Gonella and his band, blimey it was hot in Africa I wasn't prepared for that and surprisingly cold at night, I never was that keen on camping and the toilet facilities in the desert left a lot to be desired."

"Now I think about it I do remember some of the concert parties I've toured with were not the most professional performers, in fact it would be true to say some were absolutely dreadful." "I think that's where people thought of the joke about E.N.S.A being short for

Every Night Something Awful and there was always a shortage of women so the men would have to dress up as women, some looked like bad Panto Dames although a few were amazing, too convincing actually, I'm sure some of them will end up being famous, the British have always loved a man in a frock right back to the days of the music halls."

"I came home before the end of the war and performed again with Henry Hall on his Henry Hall's Rhythm Entertainment wireless show and that's pretty much all there is to tell Sir," she said.

"Then finally when the war was over, I gave up the business and trained as a secretary, somehow getting changed in dirty factories or a works canteen seemed to have lost its glamour, I got top marks in my Pitman's course you know Sir."

"Fascinating Miss Cruickshank, I'm not in the least bit surprised about that" said James, looking at the clock. "Good Lord, look at the time, you've kept us entertained longer than I noticed, time to go home I think, hopefully we've a busy day ahead of us tomorrow," and with that he handed her a set of keys for the office.

"Thank you, Sir," she said pausing and then continued. "Oh, there's just one more thing I forgot to mention, I lost my virginity during the war, I lost my virginity on quite a number of occasions you might say, you know what it's like in war when you're not sure if you'll be alive the next day, don't you Sir.

"I certainly do," said James," I certainly do, I look forward to seeing you bright and early tomorrow Miss Cruickshank."

She smiled, "Me too Sir, me too, goodnight."

THE GREASE MONKEY.

Miss Cruickshank had arrived early and after making a cup of tea had set about arranging the filing system for the office when a voice called out from halfway down the stairs.

"Put the kettle on," said George the GPO man as he entered the office.

"Good morning George," she said "and how are you this bright and early morning?"

"I'm very well Miss, I've just called in with something for the boys."

"I'm sure they will be pleased to see you George," she said, as she went to make the tea.

"Strong, no sugar," he called, as she left the office.

"I remember George, I suppose you'd like a biscuit?"

"Yes, please Miss, thank you."

Miss Cruickshank returned with the tea and a couple of biscuits which they shared, they sat and chatted for a little while until James and Archie arrived, James entered the office first.

"Good morning Miss Cruickshank," he said, "and hello to you too George and what brings you here might I enquire?"

"Good morning to you too Sir," said George. "Well Sir I came across something in the stores last night which seems to be surplus to requirements and I thought it might be of use to you?"

"What might that be?" said James.

"I've got an entire phone book collection for all of Great Britain, I thought it would be useful, it's in the back of my van outside, perhaps Mr Archie might like to bring them in?"

"What a damn good idea," said James. "Would you mind Archie."

Archie got up to get the phone books and Miss Cruickshank went to make more tea.

George reached into his bag and took out a book. "Here Sir you can have a quick look, this is A-B of the London books."

James took the book and glanced at the cover. “This is dated 1947, that’s this year George,” he paused, “surplus?”

“Well Sir, there’s surplus and there’s Nobby in the stores version of surplus,” he paused to gauge the reaction from James who had smiled and raised an eyebrow.

“Nobby said to me this morning, we can’t send these out George look at the dust on ‘em, there must be someone out there who wouldn’t mind ‘em with a bit of dust on and I immediately thought of you Sir.”

“That’s very kind of you George,” said James as he slipped a ten bob note into George’s top pocket.

“I suppose Nobby in the stores will be sufficiently remunerated for removing the dust will he George.”

“Yes Sir, of course he will, Nobby and I have an understanding,” replied George.

“Well, thank you once again George, I suppose you’d better be cutting along now, won’t they be missing you at work?”

“Oh no Sir, I’m never missed at work,” said George, “the manager and I have an understanding.”

“Why am I not surprised by that,” said Archie as he led George out of the office and when he came back Miss Cruickshank was talking to James.

"It seemed rather a strange phone call," she said. "The young man appeared to be whispering, I think he said his name was William and he would come to see you this afternoon, he finished the call rather abruptly he didn't say why he needed assistance."

"How intriguing," said James. "It looks as if we have our first client."

Later that afternoon Miss Cruickshank escorted a young man into the main office, "This is Mr William Trubshaw," she said.

Archie stood up to introduce himself, "I'm Archibald Cluff, pleased to meet you, do call me Archie and my associate is James Arbuth...."

He was sharply interrupted by James who bellowed. "Good God, it's Billy, Billy Trubshaw, how the very devil are you?"

"I haven't seen this fellow for what must be getting on for ten years now."

"Actually Sir, it's at least twelve, I was seventeen then," said Billy.

"Good Lord," exclaimed James. "Time certainly does fly, Billy here was one of my mechanics when I was racing at Brooklands in 1935."

"Hardly a mechanic sir, I just helped out a bit so to speak."

"Perhaps not a full-blown mechanic," said James. "But I thought you were a first-class grease monkey, you can always tell the minute someone picks up a spanner from the way they hold it whether they can use it properly, you were certainly a good step up from an oily rag, especially for a youngster."

"I noticed you still have the Bentley; do you still race?" enquired Billy.

"No Billy," said James. "I haven't competed since 1939, as you know the war put a stop to that, I'm sorry to say."

"Well if you ever want to start again and you need a good grease monkey, you know where to come," said Billy jokingly.

James thought back to the days when he was racing and said, "You know I just have to think about racing and I can smell the Castrol R but I think it's safe to say my racing days are over, I was a talented amateur and I won quite a few pots but the trouble with a cabinet full of trophies is someone's got to polish the ruddy things," he paused and said. "We did well Billy but my efforts now are firmly based here at Arbuthnott and Cluff Detective Agency."

Billy was dressed impeccably in a Savile Row suit and was well groomed like a wealthy gentleman would be with a particularly neat Trumpers haircut.

"That's a splendid suit," said James. "It has the look of Henry Poole if I'm not mistaken."

"Yes Sir, you have a very good eye it is a Henry Poole," said Billy.

"I think it fair then to assume that you won't have any trouble paying our fees," said James. "So how can we be of assistance to you Billy?"

"You remember my Uncle Robert, don't you?"

"Yes of course I do," replied James. "Uncle Bob?"

"That's right, Uncle Bob, well he seems to have gone missing," said Billy. "We haven't seen hide nor hair of him for getting on for a month."

"Sorry Archie," said James. "We need to fill you in on the full picture here, Billy's father and mine were good friends from years ago which is how I know him and his Uncle."

"Yes, that's right," said Billy. "It's a bit of a long story so I suppose I'd better start at the beginning."

"Strange as it might seem I was conceived on Christmas day 1917, although no-one realised that at the time, my father was back from the front, he had a slight leg wound which was sufficient to allow him a few days rest and recuperation over the Christmas period, he had a great sense of loyalty and hated to be away from his men, he thought he was letting the side down, so he went straight back after Christmas and was killed on the 12th January 1918."

"Uncle Bob, his brother inherited the entire estate and at that time Brightmoor House was mostly turned over to the State and was being used as a hospital so he managed to wangle release from the Army on compassionate grounds to come back to sort things out and to help my mother Sybil run the place."

"Uncle Bob had moved back into Brightmoor with his wife Jane," he paused. "By this time mother had realised she was pregnant and I was born in September 1918 just before the end of the war."

"Uncle Bob took everything in hand and was taking care of all of us and running the hospital and then came that awful flu epidemic after the war which lasted well over a year causing millions of deaths all round the world and sadly my mother caught it and died in August 1919."

"Blow me down Billy," said Archie. "That's quite a story, you must have missed your mother and father terribly?"

"Not really Sir," said Billy. "I was too young to have any memories of either of them and I was brought up by Uncle Bob and Aunt Jane as if I was their child, in fact I think of them as my mother and father and I know they think of me likewise, they couldn't have children of their own you see"

"Obviously you've informed the Police of your Uncle's disappearance?" asked James.

"Yes, we did about a week ago now but nothing much came of it, they sent the local Bobby round to get a description and I believe he went round the local villages asking a few questions but that was all."

"I phoned the Police only yesterday and spoke to Sergeant Collins who said that my Uncle was a grown man and had the right to go wherever he pleased and if he chose to go missing there was very little the Police could do about it, but they do want to speak to him as soon as he turns up."

"I don't suppose you have any idea where he may have gone, or what may have happened to him do you?" asked James.

"He left a note with an address which we have only just found," said Billy, "but something about it doesn't seem to ring true."

"Do you have it with you," said James.

Billy passed him the note and having read it James said, "Splendid, Archie pass me the phone book for Cornwall will you, thanks."

"He says here that he's gone to Reams Hotel, St Ives and yet no such hotel exists in St Ives," he paused, "you're sure this is his handwriting are you Billy?"

"Yes Sir, without a doubt, he has a very distinctive way of writing his g's and y's," said Billy as he was pointing to the note, "see there, where he's written, I'm going to have to go away, it's his writing without a doubt."

"I'll hang on to this note if that's alright with you." "Is there anything else you can tell us that might help in finding your Uncle?" James asked quizzically.

Billy, hesitated and then replied, "The Police are looking for him as they suspect him of murder."

"It might have been better, had you mentioned this at the beginning, don't you think," said Archie rather angrily.

James stood up and said, "Alright, Archie let's hear the man out before we jump to conclusions, I've known his Uncle for many years and I find it hard to believe he could commit murder, I must say."

"I'm sure he's innocent but there is a local farmer who has been killed and unfortunately Bob's hat was found at the scene of the crime, Billy seemed moved and said, "I don't want Uncle Bob hung, you've got to help, Sir."

"Don't worry Billy, we'll get to the bottom of this," said James, "are you sure there's nothing else you can think of that might help?"

"I don't know if it's anything," said Billy "but Uncle Bob has a motor yacht which he keeps at Folkstone harbour, it was commandeered for the Dunkirk evacuation by the Navy, well they didn't give it back until after the war and it was in a terrible state."

"It's called Blackbird and was made for him in 1938 not that long before the war, it's beautiful again now 103 ft long all brass with teak decks and oak inside, he only got her back from Goole's about a year ago after decommissioning."

"He keeps a six man crew on permanent standby so he can use her whenever he wants to, but he loves to captain her himself, it's his one major extravagance, although he does seems to have been using it more than usual, whenever he's missing lately he's out on the boat."

"Surely that's not unusual, I know if I had a boat as splendid as that I would use it as often as possible, wouldn't you Archie?" said James.

Archie nodded and smiled, "damn right, I would," he said.

"There's something that seems odd to me though, before the war we used to go on trips to France for the weekend in Blackbird, myself Uncle Bob and Aunt Jane, we had fabulous fun but recently some rather strange chaps have been seen near the boat, I'm afraid he's got mixed up in something illegal, something he can't handle." Billy paused and said, "I don't mean to be rude Sir but do you think you and Archie can handle this, I'd hate to think of either of you getting harmed, I'd rather leave it to the Police."

"Well," said James, "firstly I wouldn't advise leaving it to the Police, I imagine if they had their way they'd be chasing him for murder rather than looking for the real culprit and secondly, Archie and I were in the Commandos during the war and we're more than capable of looking after ourselves."

Archie bristled slightly and said, "Let me tell you a story Billy, I joined the Army at the very beginning and by 1940 I was a Sergeant in the Royal Artillery and I worked damn hard to get that extra stripe, it meant a lot to me, as did the pride I felt when I was picked for the Commandos."

"James and I were in different Units of the Commandos but when we met we became firm friends even though he was an Officer and I was not, he was a Captain and my Commanding Office but everyone regardless of rank has to do the same training, there's a lot of respect both ways in the Commandos, it's a damn tough Unit to be in, I'll give you an example."

"Perhaps you remember," continued Archie, "by 1942 we were losing the war in the Atlantic, the German U Boats were having a field day and then the Germans launched the Tirpitz which was an absolutely ruddy enormous Battleship with massive guns, they said its armour was a foot thick, if you took a hit from that thing you'd know all about it, can you imagine the damage a ship like that could have done had it been let loose in the Atlantic."

"Yes Sir, I remember," said Billy.

"There was only one dry dock which was large enough for the Tirpitz which was St Nazaire on the North Western coast of France and it had to be taken out of action so the Tirpitz wouldn't be able to use it, which would mean it would then have to go back to Germany for service leaving it vulnerable when it was in the open sea, so our boys in the Navy or the RAF could have a go at her."

"So they came up with a plan to destroy the 15000 ton dock gates rendering the dock unusable, however the RAF bombing wasn't accurate enough to do the job, the Navy wouldn't be able to get close enough, and there would have been no way to get sufficient explosives in place by attacking from the land so some bright spark came up with the idea that the Commandos should attack from the sea and ram the gates with a ship laden with high explosives."

"It was almost a suicide mission, they called it Operation Chariot but I think they should have called it Operation Coffin, they gave us the option not to go but most of us volunteered anyway and they asked us if we wanted to write letters to our next of kin before we went, it seemed to me an awful lot of the chaps who wrote letters didn't come back, I'm glad I didn't bother."

"Neither did I," said James, "although I must say at the time, I thought we'd be damn lucky if we got away with this one."

Archie continued, "They acquired an obsolete destroyer HMS Campbeltown, I think they must have found it in the scrap yard but they set about disguising it as a German ship by taking off two of its funnels and dumping the armour plating, just what you need when you're going on a suicide mission and about to be shot to pieces by the Germans."

"Obviously it made sense to get rid of anything heavy as it had float over the sand dunes and being packed with 4 ½ tons of Amatol high explosive which was covered by cement and steel didn't help with the weight but it was there to disguise it should the ship be boarded by the Germans but I wouldn't have minded had they left a little armour plating, just enough to stop a stray shell from exploding the Amatol might have been nice!"

"Sadly, it handled like a barge, it was desperately slow to react and with a massive turning circle but it had to do, so together with a couple of Motor Torpedo Boats and thirteen Motor Launches all made of wood each with 500 gallon petrol tanks mounted on the decks, this collection which were effectively all massive floating bombs were the vessels chosen to transport us from

Falmouth in Cornwall to St Nazaire in France."

"We had been in Falmouth for some days getting our gear stashed away on the ship and had got used to the wonderful salty smell of the sea and the fish when the fishing boats came back into harbour, it was like being on holiday at the seaside, except the holiday atmosphere wasn't going to last and we didn't have our buckets and spades."

"We set sail at 2pm on the 26th March, it was a still moonlit night and as we slowly slipped out of the harbour some of us went below to get some sleep but the Campbeltown was an old nail of a ship and you could smell the fumes from the engine everywhere on board, chaps were throwing up all over the place and even worse once we were going up the Loire as no-one was allowed on deck for fear of giving the game away, at least on the way over we managed to get on deck for a crafty fag and some salt spray on our faces."

"Thirty three awful hours later we were entering the estuary of the Loire, at least we hadn't been caught by any spotter planes during the daylight hours and the water was a lot calmer, it was a little like a gentle cruise up the river, the trees lining the banks smelled so refreshing in the cold night air, so all we had to do next was get past the 28 heavy gun emplacements, together with search lights and the 43 anti-aircraft guns in concrete emplacements on top of the submarine pens which were next to the dry dock gates."

"Oh, yes I forgot and not to get stuck on the sand dunes or caught on the submarine nets and avoiding the mines, then get off the Campbeltown set the charges and take on the 5000 Germans stationed in the town, destroy the pumps and the winding house and then attempt to escape!"

"It sounds like a piece of cake when you say it like that," said James sarcastically.

"If only," said Archie, "the ruddy RAF were supposed to assist with an air raid to distract the Germans from our actions but they were told not to attack if there was cloud cover as we didn't want any French people killed during the attack but it was cloudy and the damn planes were still flying about alerting the Germans that something was going on, it's quite amazing how much noise four Merlin engines on a Lancaster can make on a still cloudy night, there were some choice words shouted at them before they finally buggered off, I can tell you."

"Rather amazingly the first part of the mission went quite well but we did have the advantage of being disguised as a German ship complete with German flag and all the necessary passwords to signal to the shore for safe passage we just kept flashing the message, friendly ship damaged coming in for repairs and the bluff kept working for some time but obviously it wasn't going to last, eventually the Germans twigged it and all hell broke loose."

"The RAF had gone by now which helped but then the Germans switched off the searchlights which didn't help as the Captain couldn't see where he was going, it must have been hard enough steering the ruddy thing when he could see where he was going and then the Captain was hit and killed, then the chap who took over was hit, I remember thinking we're going to cop it now and then suddenly the lights came on again and they realised we were too far to port."

"Frantic steering took place on the bridge and the ship slowly lumbered to starboard striking the dock as we passed," Archie paused and laughed, "some bright spark called out, you'll never pass your driving test like that mate, but we managed to keep going and with another turn hard to port we cut through the anti-torpedo nets and rammed the dock, we must have been going at the full speed when we hit as the impact threw us to our feet and when we got up we found we'd landed 33 feet on top of the gates, it was 1.34 pm which amazingly enough was only three minutes later than scheduled"

"One of the Motor Torpedo Boats came past at one hell of a speed and shot its torpedo's into the submarine pen next to the dock gate which gave us a little cover when they exploded while we followed James who commanded our troop down the scaling ladders on the port side and ran like hell towards the winding house to place our explosives, I remember him shouting, run you bastards as we landed on the dockside and my God did we run."

"I had never been under such intense fire before, it came from every conceivable angle, you could see red and green tracer everywhere and hear it pinging off the metal bridges and the walls as we passed and sadly some men were injured and some killed as we got closer to the winding house, which was our target but we couldn't stop for them, perhaps there might be a chance to pick them up on the way out."

"Finally the mad dash inside and a brief moment of calm as the explosive chaps set their charges, it seemed to go very quiet, it was almost like being in a dream, I knelt down and a bead of sweat trickled into my eye which I wiped away, I thought at first it might be blood and my heart was pounding fit to burst, before we ran outside again in a hail of bullets, I saw James go down in front of me, he'd caught one in the leg, I could see the blood seeping through his trousers."

"Yes," said James, "I remember you said, I'm not ruddy well leaving you here mate you still owe me ten bob from the poker game and then he slung me on his back and we were away, Lord knows how he carried me all the way to the jetty but he did."

"Amazing what adrenaline can do when you're under fire," said Archie.

"We did get a little cover when the first winding house exploded, I could see men thrown in the air and thought, I hope they're Jerries, shortly followed by ours while we were attempting to secure the jetty called the Old Mole and then later a massive explosion as the pump house went up and we were showered in debris, we'd held the jetty as long as we could but eventually it was time to leave, but how?"

"As I looked out to sea all I could see was fire, it was like a vision of hell, the whole surface of the sea was on fire and as the petrol tanks on the Motor Launches went up, I could hear the men screaming on the boats, and smell the burning flesh, that's a smell you never forget."

"I thought to myself, we're not going to make it this time and then suddenly out of the fire came a launch and we all scrambled aboard, the Captain slammed the engines to full ahead and we got the hell out of there as fast as we could, there was tracer fire everywhere but we got out of the harbour with just two more minor casualties."

"We kept going and by some miracle got to the estuary in time to see HMS Atherstone firing on five German torpedo boats who made smoke and turned tail, we came along side and clambered up the cargo nets pulling the injured blokes with us and were quickly aboard and on our way home, we didn't know then whether the mission had succeeded."

"James had his leg patched up and later the Captain came to tell us that the delayed fuses on the Campbeltown had finally worked at 12.00 that day and the dry docks had been blown to pieces taking a good number of Nazis who were aboard the Campbeltown at the time with them."

"I stayed with the Commandos until the end of the war but James went on to work with SOE and then clever things with codes and ciphers where he was promoted to Major at a secret house he called B.P although at the time he said he was going to join Captain Ridley's shooting party of all things."

"Do you mind if I enquire what you did in the war?" said Archie.

"Now, now," said James I can see where you're going with this."

"No, that's alright," said Billy, "I see your point, I had a very uneventful war on anti-aircraft guns, most of it in Wales in charge of three ack-ack guns defending a flock of sheep and Cardiff docks, I wanted to do other things, to get to the real fighting but I was too damn good with the ack-ack they wouldn't let me change."

"We all serve in our own different ways Billy, I sure you've downed more German planes than Archie and myself put together," said James, "I think what Archie was trying to get across was that together we have the brawn and the brains to solve the riddle of your Uncles disappearance."

"Yes Sir, I'm confident that you do," said Billy.

"Very good Billy," said James, "in that case I think we need a little trip to Brightmoor and a chat with your local Police."

A TRIP TO BRIGHTMOOR.

James and Archie were racing down the A21 in the Bentley, the straight six engine burbling nicely as they passed through village after village and with the screen down and just the racing screens for cover Archie was having trouble holding the map but enjoying every moment of the drive.

"This should be a simple run," shouted Archie over the exhaust and wind noise, "follow the A21 then fork right at Bromley Common onto the B2026 which runs straight to Edenbridge."

"Yes indeed," replied James, "it's just a shame they removed all the signposts during the war, it doesn't help with navigation."

"Well I suppose that was the idea of it, to confuse the Germans if they had invaded" said Archie, "do you think they'll ever put them all back."

"Not with the shortage of steel we have at the moment but I expect everything will get back to normal eventually," shouted James as he double de clutched into third gear for a tight corner and as he accelerated fiercely out of the bend, the back end of the car broke away causing him to apply a fair amount of opposite lock, he laughed as he briefly remembered his racing days at Brooklands.

"Well held Sir," said Archie.

After a few more hairy moments they arrived at the Gate House of Brightmoor and drove respectfully up the drive.

"Is this house in the same county," said Archie, "we must have done half a mile already."

"Not long now," said James as they rounded a bend to reveal the house.

"Good God," said Archie, "that's not a house, it's a ruddy castle with windows, it's enormous!"

With the gravel of the forecourt crunching under the tyres of the Bentley they came to a halt at the front door of the house, stopped the engine and climbed out, the sound of the exhaust pinging as it cooled down and the smell of Castrol R in their nostrils.

Billy had come down on the train the night before and came out to greet them together with Wilson the Butler and Robert the footman, the Butler was a tall distinguished elderly man but the footman was much younger and somewhat shorter, "Hello chaps," he said, "good drive, knowing James I expect it was an interesting one."

"Come on in and have some luncheon, Wilson has prepared a cold collation do follow him to the dining room."

Billy went in and Archie and James followed Wilson, as they entered the front door, they were faced with a magnificent entrance hall with a superb ornate carved oak staircase leading to the upper floors with large paintings on every wall. "Your ancestors?" questioned Archie.

"Actually no," said Billy, "do go in for luncheon, I shall join you in a minute and I can tell you the story of the paintings." He gestured towards two large mahogany doors to their right, "I'll be with you in a moment, do make yourselves at home."

James and Archie followed Wilson the Butler who walked at a very leisurely pace and entered the dining room which was another amazing room with a wonderful decorative plaster ceiling and tall windows with silk curtains and yet more portraits on the wall and a massive dining table which was able to seat at least twenty four people, Archie was certainly impressed and said, "This is a bit posh, isn't it?"

"Yes, I suppose it is," said James, "but I've known Billy and his family for so long and he's always been here so I've become used to this being normal."

"Gentlemen, do serve yourselves, said Wilson the Butler, I shall leave you in Roberts capable hands should you require anything." He turned on his heels said, "Tickety-boo," and left the dining room.

An array of silver platters with lids was arranged on the dresser and James walked over and said to Archie, "Shall I be mum?" Raising the lids, he took a selection of cold meats and on raising the last lid was met by a number of pork pies.

"Yes please," said Archie, "I'll have two of those."

James duly obliged and having made up a plate for himself sat at the table opposite Archie who had already started, "Cracking pies," he said.

"They certainly look it," said James, "and how nice not be cramped when one is eating," which caused Archie to raise a smile.

At that moment the dining room doors opened and Billy came in followed by another footman carrying a bottle of wine, "I assume you will both be taking wine," he said as he went to the dresser and served himself and returned to sit at the head of the table.

The footman inquired if they required anything else and

Billy said, "No thank you, we'll ring if we need anything, thank you Robert."

"Is he a Butler too," asked Archie, to which Billy replied, "Oh no, that's Robert he's just a footman, Wilson is the Butler, there's only one Wilson, in more ways than one."

"You were asking about the portraits," continued Billy, "well it all started with my Grandfather Herbert who was born in Clapham and came from fairly humble beginnings, his father had a small grocer's shop which he inherited when his father died."

"Coming from such humble roots I think it safe to say Grandfather Herbert was a driven man, he worked every hour there was, this was in the days of the Victorian Golden Years, it was the days of the industrial revolution and the rise of the middle class and he built his business up until he finally opened the department store in Knightsbridge in 1865."

"Store in Knightsbridge?" said Archie.

"Yes Hamwells, that was Herbert too," said Billy, "how silly of me, of course you didn't know, he called it Hamwells because he thought it had a nice upper class ring to it and I must say it certainly did have, he made a fortune and that's why none of the pictures in the hall are our ancestors, as Grandfather would have said, the pictures came as a job lot with the house so to speak."

"I think it was two or three years after he opened Hamwells that he bought Brightmoor, got it at a knock down price by all accounts, bought it lock stock and barrel, the previous owner was Lord Eddleton, his son had drunk and gambled excessively, but his father was a very honourable man and kept paying his debts until finally the estate was bankrupt and he had no option but to sell up, rather sad really."

"Grandfather said he did his best for them and gave them a small cottage on the estate at a peppercorn rent but it didn't work out, Lord Eddleton was getting on and I think the shock of it was too much for him and he died soon after, his wife remained in the cottage until her death some years later."

"How very sad," said James.

"It certainly was," said Billy, "I have no idea what happened to the feckless son there was a rumour that he had drunk himself to death," he paused for a moment and then continued, "anyway Grandfather spent a small fortune on the house as during the ownership of Lord Eddleton a considerable amount of it had fallen into disrepair and when Grandfather died it went to my father Richard."

"This was in 1911 and father took control of Hamwells and the estate but then the war came along and both he and Uncle Bob joined up."

"Why didn't they stay at home, surely they might have

been able to stay to run the business?" asked Archie.

"Yes, they might have done but both my father and Uncle Bob had a very strong sense of duty," Billy paused, "don't forget these were the days when young ladies would give white feathers to men who they thought were shirking and initially everyone thought it would be all over by Christmas."

"As I said yesterday, I was conceived when father was home on leave December 1917 and then he was killed the next month, on the 12th January 1918, such a shame he got so close to the end of the war and didn't make it but I know there were chaps who were actually killed on the very last day."

"It was a tragic time with so many dead, can you imagine what mother must have been going through, to lose her husband and then having to deal with Brightmoor and Hamwell's going to Uncle Bob."

"Weren't you upset by that after all had you have been born it all would have been yours?" asked Archie.

"No Sir," said Billy, "Thank God Uncle Bob was here to take care of mother, he looked after her until her unfortunate death in the flu epidemic in August 1919 and has looked after me all my life and the estate will all come to me when Uncle Bob dies, it's in his will."

"And you trust him with that do you Billy," enquired Archie.

"I would trust Uncle Bob with my life," he paused, "with my life Sir."

"I'm sure you would Billy," said James, "exactly how big is the estate, you don't think there is someone here who may have had a grudge against Uncle Bob, a disgruntled employee, perhaps?

"The estate must be 27 thousand acres which obviously covers the grounds here, the rest is mostly farmland which we farm ourselves," he thought for a moment and then continued, "together with some 30 or so tenant farmers and the village of Edenbridge and that's just the estate, so if you're looking for someone with a grudge you've an awful lot of people to choose from."

"I know it might seem a little flippant," said Billy, "but if you consider Hamwells and any disgruntled employee or business rival, plus Whintons Engineering which Uncle Bob purchased in 1931, you're effectively looking for a needle in a haystack."

"Whintons Engineering? Said Archie, "Obviously your Uncle Bob took after his father."

"I'm sure you're right," said Billy, "Uncle Bob is a very astute businessman and an extremely wealthy man, he was a trained engineer before he took over the estate, he purchased Whintons in the depression of the thirties, it was going bankrupt and he got it for a song, I know he always used to joke he got it for less than a decent lunch at his club, although that was a joke, I know it was ridiculously cheap."

"Do you know what happened to the previous owner?" asked James.

"I'm afraid not," replied Billy, "but Uncle Bob kept the workers on, he even paid them whilst the factory was being modernised and then of course he kept it ticking over until the war came along and he made another fortune, they specialised in bearings but they could turn their hand to anything that involved engineering, he is a very canny businessman."

James stood up and said, "Thank you Billy, most enlightening, now I wonder if we might go to our rooms for a while I'd like to freshen up, it was quite some drive this morning."

"Certainly" said Billy as he led them out of the dining room and gestured to the footman, "just follow Robert he will show you to your room, we sound the gong for dinner and don't worry Archie we won't be dressing formally tonight, we only bother with that nowadays when The King visits!"

Archie was unsure whether he was being serious but laughed anyway.

"Would it be possible to put the Bentley in the garage it looks like rain and it saves having to put the tonneau cover on." asked James.

"Certainly, it's around the back you can't miss it," replied Billy, "if the doors are closed just give them a knock, William the chauffeur should be around and he will let you in."

They followed Robert who showed them to their rooms and they went in, Archie was most impressed as he wandered round the room and paused at another door which he opened and was slightly surprised to see James standing on the other side.

"Very useful when you're having an affair if you get invited to a house party," said James.

"I'll make a note of that should I ever get invited," smiled Archie quizzically.

James continued, "some houses used to ring a bell at six in the morning before everyone got up to give those who wanted or needed the opportunity to return to their own rooms!"

"When you have a moment take the Bentley round to the garage will you Archie," said James as he handed him the key, "you never know what you might find out with a quick chat with the chauffeur."

"I'll see what I can do," said Archie.

Having washed the dust from his face he set about taking the Bentley to the garage, she started on the button and he drove gently round to garage which had a series of arched doors all of which were shut and a floor above with small windows, so he gave a quick blast on the hooter which caused William the chauffeur to poke his head out, “Sorry to keep you waiting Sir and how can I help you,” said William “I was upstairs, that’s where my quarters are.”

“That’s fine,” said Archie, “I understand we can park the car in the garage.”

“Certainly Sir, I’ll open the doors if you’d like to back in that would be perfect.”

Archie backed the Bentley into the garage, switched off and climbed out, there was a wonderful smell of engine oil and new leather from the collection of vehicles stored within.

“Very nice car, Sir,” said William, “yours, is it?”

“No, it belongs to my friend Mr Arbuthnott but you have a rather nice selection in here too,” said Archie pointing to a Daimler limousine, a Rolls-Royce shooting brake, an MG TA and what appeared to be a brand-new Bentley Mk VI.

“Will you and Mr Arbuthnott be down for the weekend Sir, I could give her a wash and polish while you’re here if you like,” said William.

“Thank you, William, I’m sure Mr Arbuthnott would like that.”

"I was just admiring the Daimler limousine and the Rolls-Royce shooting brake, why the Daimler and not another Rolls-Royce," said Archie, "if you don't mind me asking?"

"Fashion I believe Sir, the Royal Family favour Daimler motors and I think others just follow suite, don't get me wrong it's a very nice car to drive, straight six nearly six litres so it's fairly relaxing to drive but I think I'd probably go for a Royce if it was my choice."

"What about the Rolls-Royce shooting brake?" asked Archie, "that looks like quite a substantial vehicle."

"It certainly is Sir, it's been in the family since 1930 we use it for shooting parties and picking guests and their luggage from the station, the engine's nearly eight litres, it's built like a tank, said William, "in fact during the First World War they covered earlier Royce's in armour plating and mounted a gun on them which effectively turned it into a tank."

"I must say the wood's in beautiful condition," said Archie.

"I do my best to look after all the cars here Sir," replied William.

Glancing at the two-seater sports MG TA Archie said, "I must say the MG looks a little out of place in here?"

"It belongs to Mrs Trubshaw," said William, "you can

often see her buzzing along the lanes visiting friends and the like."

"Wow," said Archie, "that's a brand-new Bentley isn't it, I assume that belongs to Mr Billy Trubshaw, he's done well to get hold of one of those especially with the shortage of steel and the Government export or die policy, they say it's not what you know but who you know."

"Yes Sir very true," said William, "they only started making them last year in 1946, we got her in December of that year, I believe it cost over four thousand pounds including purchase tax and Mr Billy said he'd been offered twice that for her but he wouldn't sell her, you have to be fairly well off to be able to do that Sir."

"You do indeed," said Archie as he noticed a small rack of shotguns hanging on the wall, "do they use those for the shoot," asked Archie who was more used to the Army way of doing things where they kept strict control on who had access to the guns.

"Oh no Sir, they keep the expensive Purdy's and the like locked up inside the house, these are just here for anyone to use for killing rats and vermin, or the occasional badger that sort of thing."

"I'm surprised they aren't locked away more securely," said Archie, "anyone could use them."

"That's the general idea Sir," said William, "that's why

they leave the cheap guns here and lock the expensive ones away, I can't imagine anyone wanting to steal them and I'm here most of the time except when I'm driving and then I lock the doors, my quarters as you know are above the garage, there's only myself and Wilson who have a key, they're perfectly safe Sir."

"I see," said Archie, "thanks for your help, I enjoyed looking at the cars."

"My pleasure Sir," said William.

"Goodbye," said Archie as he left the garage and walked back to the house the gravel crunching under his feet. "Not the sort of surface to try to creep up behind someone on a Commando raid," he thought.

Later that evening Archie heard the gong sound downstairs and rushed to the connecting door to speak to James, "Can you give me a hand with these cufflinks, I don't want to be late for dinner I'm nervous enough already without turning up late for parade," he said panicking.

"Don't worry," replied James, "that was just the dressing gong, there's plenty of time left."

Half an hour later the dinner gong sounded and James and Archie made their way down the magnificent staircase and entered the dining room where Billy greeted them and placed them at the table side by side and then sat back down at the head of the table.

“I thought they said, they don’t make a fuss dressing for dinner,” said Archie under his breath to James, “there’s so many servants in this room dressed in penguin suits I feel like I’m at the zoo.”

One of them, was the tall elderly gentleman who they recognised as the Butler, he addressed James and Archie. “Good evening gentlemen, if you require anything during your stay please do ask one of the staff and we’ll be only too happy to oblige, we do like everything to be tickety-boo,” he paused for a moment and said, “yes, tickety-boo, Sir, tickety-boo, will you be taking wine.”

They both said yes and Wilson gestured to a footman who duly filled their glasses, he then continued towards the dining room doors which were opened to reveal a woman in a stunning green cocktail dress, she had an air of class about her which one normally finds with old money and Billy, James and Archie stood up as she walked to the table.

Although her hair was grey, she was impeccably turned out and was extremely thin and was wearing fashionable silk seamed stockings of the finest denier and a large diamond necklace that sparkled in the light of the dining room.

“Good evening Madam,” said Wilson as he seated her opposite James and Archie.

“If that’s not dressing for dinner,” Archie whispered, “I

hate to think what she'd look like if she had made an effort!"

Billy introduced Aunt Jane to James and Archie and they started dinner, which caused Archie to comment to James, "There's so much cutlery here I've no idea where to start."

"Just start at the outside and work your way in," replied James.

"This certainly is a stunning house, Mrs Trubshaw," said Archie nervously.

"Do please call me Jane," she said, "yes, it is magnificent and one day it will be up to Billy to look after it, for you never really own a house like this, one is merely a custodian until the next generation have their turn."

She turned and looked James in the eye and said, "I'm so glad you have come to help us find Bob, from what Billy has told me I feel we are in safe hands."

"We'll certainly do our best Jane I can promise you that," said James, "I don't suppose you can think of any reason why he may have disappeared."

"I'm praying nothing awful has happened to him, although I would have thought he would have tried to contact me and if he has gone into hiding and that worries me, just who is he hiding from and why, we have no enemies that I'm aware of?"

“That does seem to be the case at the moment,” said James “but we will get to the bottom of it I can assure you, although we do seem to have a very large haystack in which to find the needle” he paused “if you don’t mind me asking, what about the farmer he’s alleged to have killed?”

“Utter rubbish,” snapped Jane, “Bob didn’t do that, I know he didn’t,” she hesitated for a moment but was obviously upset, “Bob would never have killed anyone with a shot gun, it’s far too messy for a start and if he’d wanted to kill someone he’d have used a hunting rifle, you want a clean shot for that sort of thing, no it definitely wasn’t Bob.”

“I must say, I’m inclined to agree with you,” said Archie, “ I’ve never fired a shotgun, I’ve fired an awful lot of other guns in my time in the Commandos but you’re right, no-one would use a shotgun unless that was the only gun available to them”.

“We’ll have to see to that,” said Jane, “Billy can arrange to have a few clays throw up for you in the morning, just for fun, you’ll soon see why the hunting rifle is a much better option.”

“That’s very kind of you Jane,” said Archie, “I look forward to it.”

“I’m off to bed now,” said Jane, “you boys go into the smoking room for a nightcap and I will see you in the morning, goodnight.”

The boys stood up as she left the room and they made their way to the smoking room which was laid out with two large sofas which were at right angles to a very large and imposing fireplace on one wall and the opposing wall was completely covered with book shelves set out as a library with the same wonderful ceiling as in the dining room, Wilson the butler and Robert the footman were waiting with a decanter of port and some glasses. Wilson enquired, "will that be all Sir?"

"Yes, thank you that will be all tonight Wilson," said Billy as he offered James and Archie some rather splendid Corona cigars.

"Tickety-boo," said Wilson as he exited the room, "Goodnight gentlemen."

They chatted together for some time and having finished their cigars and port, James said, "time for bed I think, we've a clay shoot in the morning and I'd like to arrange to see the Police Inspector tomorrow too."

They went up together and at the top of the stairs, as they went towards their own rooms Billy said, "goodnight chaps, see you tomorrow."

Archie and James said, "goodnight," and James continued, "don't worry old chap tomorrow is another day, we'll get there, you'll see, goodnight."

A DAY SHOOTING.

James knocked on the adjoining bedroom door and when Archie appeared, he said, "Good morning, and how are we getting on with the tweed?"

"Not well, I had a ruddy awful night's sleep," replied Archie, "I'm not used to it being so quiet when I'm trying to get to sleep, it took me ages to get off, I'm just glad they didn't have to ring the early bell or I'd have had no sleep at all."

"I know you said the agency is aiming for the upper crust clients but I hadn't realised it would entail quite so much fancy attire, I thought the plus fours were a bit fiddly but I don't think I'll be on jankers for my uniform, what do you think?"

Archie stood in front of the full-length mirror and admired himself, he was dressed in very fetching Harris Tweed suit, together with plus four trousers. "I don't know, perhaps I could get used to all this," said Archie as he looked himself up and down, "although you don't have to be dressed up to fire a gun and kill someone as we both know from experience."

"Yes," said James, "but we are now at Brightmoor and one has to be seen to be correctly attired for shooting or riding or dinner, you should see how many times they change during the day when they have Royalty staying, he wasn't joking about The King!"

"I dare say they probably do have an outfit for killing people down here in the country," said Archie, "I wonder what it looks like?"

"You're wearing it now, Archie," said James, "and it looks very smart but we'd better get a move on, we don't want to be keeping them waiting," he opened the door and said, "after you old man," as they made their way downstairs.

"I think you might enjoy breakfast," said James as they descended the stairs and headed to the dining room, "I thought I could smell kedgeree."

"Smells like curry to me," said Archie who was a man who preferred the plainer English foods like a steak and kidney pie. "What's in it?"

"Well," said James, "the recipe varies but basically it's fish, generally haddock boiled rice, hard boiled eggs, parsley, curry powder and butter, it originated in India and was brought back by British Colonials in the Victorian times, it's jolly good"

"I'll give it a go," said Archie, "don't want to appear rude, do we, anyway this country air has given me an appetite, I'm starving, I could eat a horse!"

He piled his plate high and sat down at the table next to James.

"Morning chaps," said Billy, who was sitting in his usual place at the top of the table, "sleep well?"

"Archie didn't do so well," said James, "he's not used to it being so quiet but I slept like a log, thanks."

Billy glanced at Archie who by now had nearly finished his kedgeree. "You look like you enjoyed that he said, "do go round again if you're peckish."

"I will Sir, if you don't mind," said Archie as he headed of for another large helping of kedgeree.

"I spoke to the local Police this morning, I said we'd drop in later today," said Billy, "but first I've had Angus our Estate Manager set up a clay shoot on the small paddock so Archie can try his hand with a shotgun, I think he'll enjoy himself, the Royce will be out the front for you whenever you're ready."

When they had all finished breakfast James and Archie went outside to find the Rolls-Royce shooting brake was waiting for them, as immaculate as when Archie saw it in the garage, footmen were loading wicker hampers into the rear and a rather diminutive Scotsman also dressed in hunting tweeds introduced himself.

"Good morning gentlemen," he said, "my name's Angus and I hope you will enjoy the mornings shooting, if there's anything you require please don't hesitate to ask."

As they said their thanks, Billy appeared at the front door. "Everybody ready," he said, "good, let's crack on then."

He opened the back door of the Royce and gestured to James and Archie to get in. "I'll be in the back with you chaps and Angus will be riding in the front with William."

The Royce had such a large slow revving engine that the only discernible sound you could hear as it slowly drove off, was the gravel crunching under its tyres. "Nice engine," thought James.

The small paddock was a few miles away and when they drove into the paddock it was set out for a shoot, with the trap for firing the clays in the air set behind some bales of hay and a rather large marquee together with tables and chairs and a fine white linen tablecloth.

Billy jumped out of the car first and set about organising things, "won't be a mo chaps," he said and soon appeared again at the car door and poking his head inside said, "ready chaps, then let's go."

They both followed Billy to the shooting area and Angus came and gave them their guns, "I'm sure you know how to handle a gun Sir," he said to Archie, "what with your experience in the war, the only advice I would give is to aim in front of the bird and you'll be fine."

"Bird?" said Archie. "I thought we were shooting clays?"

"Yes of course we are Sir," said Angus. "I'm sorry, we still call them birds even when they're clays, what I suggest is you go first, just so you can get the feel of the gun and then we'll all take a turn." "Just call pull when you're ready and if you miss, we'll call bird away or kill if you hit it, we'll be putting up two at once, so you have to have your wits about you Sir."

Archie said, "thank you I'm ready," and then called, "Pull".

"Bird away," called Angus and for another five or six shots until Archie shattered his first clay.

"I've got it now," said Archie and continued for another twenty minutes hitting virtually all the clays sent up for him and then it was Billy's turn.

Whilst Billy was shooting, James took the opportunity to chat to Angus. "Have you worked for the family for a long time," he inquired.

"Yes Sir, I've been here years, I originally came as

Gamekeeper and was lucky enough to step up to the position of Estate Manager when Mr George the previous manager died."

"How do you find working for them, you must have seen some comings and goings in your time, I'm just trying to get some sort of idea why Mr Trubshaw might have disappeared?"

"I know exactly what you're asking," replied Angus, "and believe me Sir, if I had anything which I thought might help I would have come to you with it by now, the Trubshaws are exemplary employers, they are kind and fair, I have never had a problem with them in any way shape or form."

"Everything we do with the Estate is completely and utterly above board, there have never been any underhand dealings ever, I wish in some respects there had been, at least then I might have had something which could be helpful."

"We do see the odd character around the Estate from time to time but mostly they are tramps and just passing through, believe me Sir, if I see or hear anything which I think may be of use I will come straight to you with it."

"Thank you, Angus," said James.

"I think it must be your turn now Sir," said Angus as he led James back to the shoot and handed him a gun.

"Enjoy your shooting Sir."

When James had finished Billy said, "Good fun wasn't it chaps, it's great for keeping your hand in especially when shooting's out of season."

"On the subject of shooting gentlemen," said Angus, "Mr Trubshaw has asked me to set up a demonstration for you, if you'd care to follow me." He led them to the other side of the paddock where a number of pumpkins had been arranged on top of some straw bales.

Angus took the shotgun he was carrying, loaded it and said, "This is the same bird shot you've just been using," he raised the gun and shot first one barrel and then the second causing the two pumpkins to fall to the ground intact but full of bird shot.

Just then Aunt Jane appeared immaculately turned out in riding jodhpurs and riding boots, even though she was a little older you could tell she must have been quite a stunning looking woman in her youth, she was carrying a hunting rifle with telescopic sights and said, "Good morning gentlemen I trust you enjoyed your shoot."

"Very much," said Archie, "it's been most informative."

"I think I might be able to add to your knowledge," said Aunt Jane as she raised her rifle, briefly paused and then fired two shots in quick succession and hit the remaining two pumpkins which shattered on impact.

"Good Lord," said Archie, "that's some shooting."

"Thank you," said Jane, "both Bob and I have won medals for our shooting, we wouldn't try to kill someone with a shotgun, a clean shot with a decent hunting rifle, that's the way to do it." "Now, time for luncheon I think," she said as she walked back to the marquee.

As they sat down to dine Wilson and the footmen served them attentively, the table was awash with food and drink.

"You don't go short down here in the country, do you?" said Archie.

"That's the great advantage of living in the countryside," said Billy, "if you can't grow it, you can go out and shoot it, there's always a rabbit or pigeon to be had."

"And everyone has a gun," said Archie.

"I wouldn't say everyone," replied Billy, "but you are right, it's not hard to lay your hands on a shotgun in the country."

Everybody ate well and Archie said, "well I'm stuffed, I couldn't eat another thing."

"Very good Sir," said Wilson, "tickety-boo."

Aunt Jane stood up and addressed the table, "I suggest

we take the Daimler and visit the wretched Police, although what good it will do, I have no idea."

"That will be all thank you Wilson, you may use the shooting brake to return."

"Tickety-boo madam," said Wilson.

The Daimler was a very large limousine so Billy and Aunt Jane sat in the rear seats and Archie and James sat on fold down seats in front of them.

As they were driving towards Edenbridge Archie said, "I hope you don't mind me asking Billy, but I couldn't help noticing your Butler keeps saying tickety-boo which seems a rather strange expression for a Butler."

"A little odd, perhaps," replied Aunt Jane, "it's a strange affectation he picked up many years ago when the Duke of Windsor used to come to stay and it's somehow stuck, actually he's been doing it for so long we hardly notice now."

"You must have known the Duke of Windsor fairly well?" asked Archie.

Aunt Jane said, "Yes we did, he used to come to Brightmoor on a fairly regular basis," she stared out of the car window for a moment as if remembering and then replied, "I think it fair to say he was a bit of a ladies man in those days, he had a bit of a penchant for the married ones, of course in those days he was still The

Prince of Wales." "I found him rather charming and exceptionally stylish, he was fairly short but very well proportioned, not an ounce of fat on him, I always thought he was the type of chap who could look good if he were dressed in a sack." "He used to wear the Glenurquhart Check suits, so much so that it became known as The Prince of Wales check, I remember one weekend when he was down he had the most wonderful suit, it was almost orange in colour but very large bright check and plus fours, he had style all his own and set the trend for many to try to emulate, although many failed trying."

"He used to enjoy coming to Brightmoor, away from the prying eyes of his father or the press, he could bring whomsoever he chose and enjoy the privacy, he bought many a young woman and we were very discreet."

"I must say though, the first time we met Mrs Wallice Simpson, I think it must have been 1931 and I have to say it was a bit of a surprise, even though we were living in slightly more enlightened times it was not really De Rigueur for a future King to be having an affair with a twice married American divorcee."

"What did you think of her?" asked James.

"Pardon me," said Aunt Jane as she blew down the communication tube to the chauffeur William, "I'd like to visit the Johnsons farm while we're down this way, I'm sure you can remember the way William."

"Yes Madam," said William.

"Sorry about that," said Jane, "it's just that I've been meaning to visit for the last two or three days, they've had a horse down with colic, so I just thought I'd pop in and see how they're getting on."

"They still use horses?" questioned Archie who was after all a townie and knew little of country ways.

"Of course they do," said Billy, "there's plenty of working horses round these parts, we'd be lost without them, although we are trying to modernise it's not easy, tractors are expensive and there are plenty of farmers set in their ways who'd hate to have to give up their horses."

As the Daimler entered the farmyard some chickens scattered and a dog could be heard barking round the back of the barn and as the car drew to a halt, the barn door opened and a ruddy faced man with a large ginger beard appeared carrying a shot gun, which he promptly leaned against the wall of the barn when he realised who had come to visit.

"Good day Johnson," said Jane.

"Good day Ma'am," said farmer Johnson, " I didn't realise it be you, we've had some rum'uns round 'ere recent, Old Tom over yonder caught one sleeping in his barn 'e didn't know what 'e was a'ter as 'e ran off afore he could fetch his gun."

"You can't be too careful," said Jane, "nothing stolen, I hope?"

"No, nothing Ma'am but Old Tom said the young feller was dressed too smart for a tramp."

"I'm sure you'll keep your eyes out, shall I tell Sergeant Collins when I see him?" said Jane.

"Wouldn't hurt to tell 'im, thank you Ma'am," replied Johnson, "I wouldn't bother with new Inspector though."

"Why would that be then?" asked Jane.

"He's one of them clever buggers, been sent down 'ere from London, 'e don't fit in from what I've heard, them from town never do Ma-am."

"Thank you for that Johnson, I look forward to meeting the new Inspector we're calling in to the Police Station later, forewarned is forearmed as they say." She paused thoughtfully and then continued, "well, obviously I've popped in to see Shorty, how's he getting on?" asked Jane.

"Not so bad," replied Johnson as he led them into the barn to reveal a massive plough horse of at least 17 hands high.

"Thank you, for sending veterinary Ma'am."

"It's the least we could do Johnson," said Jane, "we

can't have our tenants losing their horses can we?"

"No Ma'am, no horse, no farm," said Johnson.

"Was it colic, as I thought," asked Jane, "I've seen horses go down with colic before, he's a fine beast and I must say looking a lot better than when I last saw him"

"Yes, veterinary said colic and to keep 'im moving, gentle though, don't give 'im cold water and 'e showed me 'ow to make a bran mash for 'im to eat and it seems to 'av done the trick." said Johnson.

Jane went over and stroked the horse and said, "all that looking after and a lot of love certainly has got Shorty back to his old self, I'm so pleased for you."

"Yes, thank you Ma'am, a little bit of love never did no-one no 'arm," said Johnson.

"Yes, indeed Johnson, a little bit of love never hurt anyone," said Jane. "Well we've got to cut along now, do keep well and if you do require anything more just send word to the big house."

Farmer Johnson said, "thank you, Ma'am," walked back with them all to the car and waved as they departed.

"Wasn't that a wonderful animal?" said Jane.

"Do you mean Johnson or the horse?" quipped Archie.

Jane smiled and said, "both!"

Archie was slightly surprised at the relationship between Jane and farmer Johnson and said, "you look after your tenants exceptionally well don't you Jane?"

"It's the way in the countryside Archie," she said.

"Now, I'm sorry for the slight interruption, James you were asking earlier what I thought of Wallis Simpson," said Jane.

"Surprisingly, I found her utterly charming, she had a ready wit, a sharp sense of humour and I thought her most sincere and the servants liked her which I've always thought was a good recommendation for anybody," she paused and then continued, "no lesser person than Winston Churchill thought that she was good for Edward, I think they were well suited, but that's just my opinion there were plenty who were far less kind, but the old school High Society were never going to accept her which I always thought to be a shame."

"It was said that the King had said of his son Edward; After I'm dead the boy will ruin himself within twelve months," she hesitated, "I have to say I felt very sorry for him as I could not see there being a good outcome to all this, I was led to believe that he and Wallis were even followed by the Metropolitan Police Special Branch."

"Then his father George V died in January 1936 and Edward became King and he said he wanted to marry

Wallis but the establishment wouldn't have it but their relationship wasn't general knowledge then and Wallis thought it might be better to be discreet and just continue as lovers."

"Edward was adamant that he wanted to marry and so in November when Wallis had obtained her Decree Nisi, he went to the Prime Minister Stanley Baldwin and announced his plan to marry, but The Government refused saying it was impossible as the Church of England was opposed, as it was morally wrong to remarry after divorce and the people would not accept an American as his wife, I'm not sure which they disliked more, being divorced or being American!"

"Winston Churchill came up with a scheme called the Cornwall Plan whereby it was suggested that Wallis might be called the Duchess of Cornwall, but would not be able to become Queen which was also rejected and then in December 1936, as our American cousins might say; The shit really hit the fan."

"Up until then the general public had no idea of all this going on and when they found out there was uproar, I don't think the establishment expected the people to be so supportive, the Daily Mail had a headline at the time which declared; The People Want Their King, unfortunately it wasn't to be."

"By this time Edward had decided to abdicate and on the night of 11th December he made a worldwide radio broadcast, in which he said; I have found it impossible to carry the heavy burden of responsibility and to discharge my duties as King as I would wish to do without the help and support of the woman I love." "I remember he added; the decision was mine and mine alone."

"I always thought it was wrong, he was so very much in love with her and even though they married I'll always think he would have made a good King, even though his brother George made a splendid fist of it, but Edward was my friend."

"He made some unfortunate errors later, especially visiting Germany but he was never a Nazi as some portrayed him, I'm sure it was just that he was in favour of appeasement with Hitler, after all who wants to go to war if you can avoid it?"

"Once again the establishment got involved and they packed him off to be the Governor of the Bahamas and to keep him well out of the way, they live in Paris now, I think they feel they are not wanted here anymore, such a shame."

"Are you in contact at all?" inquired Archie.

"No, not really, not like the old days" said Aunt Jane, " just Christmas cards, that sort of thing, too much water has flown under the bridge, but that's life I suppose," she paused and slowly continued, "I can understand why he did it, for I would have killed if someone had tried to have keep me from the man I loved, I would have killed."

THE NEW POLICE INSPECTOR.

It was a wonderful summers day as they drove through the lanes towards Edenbridge, the hedgerows were full of wild flowers and the fields were a mass of differing colours, from the purple of the lavender to the alternate browns of the wheat, corn and hemp and the green tops of the beet and turnips, all contrasting with the bright red soil of the fields which had been left fallow.

"Oh, to be in England," said James wistfully.

"Pardon?" said Archie.

"Home-Thoughts from Abroad by Robert Browning," said James.

"With its oft misquoted second line; Now that Spring is here!" said Jane smiling.

James started again, “Oh, to be in England,” and Jane continued.

Now that April’s there,

And whoever wakes in England

Sees, some morning, unaware,

That the lowest boughs and the brushwood sheaf

Round the elm-tree bole are in tiny leaf,

While the Chaffinch sings on the orchard bough

In England-now!

They all clapped and Archie said, “Here’s one for you, one I always thought of just before we went into action in the war.”

If I should die, think only this of me:

That there’s some corner of a foreign field

That is forever England.

“Yes,” said James, “Rupert Brooke, written when he was in the Navy in the 14-18 War, bizarrely enough he died of blood poisoning from an infected mosquito bite when he was in the Navy travelling to Gallipoli, I believe he’s buried somewhere out there.”

“Skyros,” said Jane.

"Pardon?" said Archie questioningly.

"Skyros, the Greek island of Skyros, that's where he's buried."

"You know everything Aunt Jane," said Billy.

"Not everything," said Jane, "but I just happen to remember it was mentioned when the poem was published in 1915, it was only just about a year since I had married Bob and it always made me think of him and hope he was safe."

"It's in times of war," said James, "that we realise what is precious and what we hold dear."

"Or times of trouble," said Jane.

"Yes indeed," said James, "perhaps we'll get some information when we see the new Inspector, let's hope so."

The Police Station in Edenbridge was a rather ramshackle building in the middle the village and Jane asked William, "Will you just stop in the square while we pop into the Police Station."

"Shall I wait, madam?" asked William as they were all getting out of the Daimler.

"Yes please," she replied, "perhaps you'd like to wait in The Blue Boar over there, we may be some time, I'm afraid."

William said, “thank you madam,” and headed off towards the pub as the others went towards the Police Station.

As they walked a young woman coming the other way stopped and said, “morning Sir, morning Madam.”

“Good day,” said Jane and turned to Billy. “This is Mrs Miller, her husband has just taken over the farm at Haxted from his father, I don’t think you’ve met her yet have you.”

“No, I haven’t yet,” said Billy, “but I have met your husband, how are you settling in, well I trust.”

“Well Sir, thank you,” she said. “Pardon me for asking, but do you have any news on Mr Trubshaw.”

“Nothing at the moment,” said Jane, “I’m sure there’s nothing to worry about but thank you for your concern, do forgive us but we have to get on,” and with that she continued to the Police Station.

Once out of earshot of Mrs Miller she turned to Billy and said, “It doesn’t take long for word to get round, does it?”

“It seems not,” said Billy as they entered the Station and went up to the desk where the Desk Sergeant was standing.

“Good day Sergeant Collins,” said Jane, “and how are we today, still having trouble with your lumbago?”

"Good day to you Madam," said Sergeant Collins. "So kind of you to inquire of my lumbago, as you know I'm a martyr to my back especially in the colder months but I have to say it's not been too bad of late, my wife has been applying the mustard compress as you suggested and it seems to be doing the trick, thank you Madam."

"I suppose you're here to see the Inspector," he said as he called for Constable Lamb. "Just follow Constable Lamb he'll show you to the Inspectors office."

Aunt June thanked Sergeant Collins and added, "Oh Sergeant, I just thought I'd mention when I called in to see farmer Johnson this morning he did tell me he'd seen a suspicious looking character hanging about, he said he looked too smart to be a tramp but I said I would mention it to you anyway."

"Thank you for that Madam, I'll make a note of that in the book and let the Constables know to keep a lookout when they're out and about."

"This way Madam," said Constable Lamb as he led them down the corridor to a door with a wooden plaque with the name Inspector Andrews engraved on it hanging by a piece of string on a nail and knocking on the door he called out. "Mrs Trubshaw to see you Sir."

A voice from the other side replied, "Enter," and they all went in to see a slightly portly and shabbily dressed man seated at his desk, he was the sort of fellow one felt would still manage to look like a sack of potatoes tied up with string had he been dressed in the finest from Savile Row.

The office was fairly small and from the look of the shelves was normally the stationary cupboard, the Inspector rose from his desk as they entered. "Good afternoon Madam, do please take a seat," he said gesturing to a chair in front of the desk, "I'm afraid you other gentlemen will have to stand, as you can see I'm a little short of space, this is just temporary until they've cleared out the old Inspectors office."

They all shuffled in and Archie attempted to close the door behind them but thought better of it as he didn't want to injure anyone in the crush.

"I was hoping to see Inspector Peters," said Jane, "as you will learn Inspector we don't like change for change's sake in the country, he was a good man and had been here for many years, I knew he was retiring but I hadn't expected him to go quite so soon."

"Yes Madam," he said, "I'm his replacement and I became available sooner than expected so they sent me down here straight away."

"I see, Inspector," said Jane repeating, "straight away, you make it sound as if they thought we were in dire need of your services Inspector, or were they that keen to be rid of you in London."

"I couldn't possibly say Madan," said the Inspector.

"I'm sure you'll fit in here nicely, once you've been here for ten years or so," said Jane, "this is the countryside Inspector, as I said they're not quick to embrace change here."

"I shall bear that in mind Madam, I'm sure it won't take that long," said the Inspector, "now I assume you are Mrs Trubshaw, but it was your husband Mr Robert Trubshaw that I was hoping to see."

"Yes, I'm Jane Trubshaw and my husband Bob is, as you know unfortunately not available at the moment, this is young Billy Trubshaw and these gentlemen are friends of the family, they are James Arbuthnott and Archibald Cluff and they are Private Detectives."

"I don't think there's any need for Private Detectives," said Inspector Williams, "I'm sure I am more than capable of dealing with the situation, I have dealt with murder cases before Madam."

"With all due respect Inspector, I was not referring to a murder, I was concerned about the disappearance of my husband," said Jane, "please tell me if you can what exactly have you done to find my husband?"

Inspector Andrews spluttered, "well I've had my Constables ask around the area but I'm afraid I have nothing to report."

Jane leaned forward in her chair and spoke softly, "nothing to report, indeed!"

"I'm afraid," replied Inspector Williams tentatively, "I'm afraid, as has been said before, your husband is an adult and as such he can go where he pleases and unfortunately, he has been connected with the murder of farmer Smith."

"I can tell you quite categorically Inspector that my husband has had nothing whatsoever to do with the murder of Mr Smith or any other farmer for that matter and what possible motive would he have for such a crime I ask you?"

Once again, the Inspector hesitated, "I'm led to believe there was some sort of confrontation between the two of them and don't forget your husband's hat was found at the scene of the crime."

"I was told farmer Smith was murdered with a shotgun and believe me Inspector I know my husband well enough to know he wouldn't murder anyone with a shotgun, especially when he has access to some of the finest hunting rifles one can buy," said Jane, "and as for his hat perhaps it was planted, there will be a logical explanation for the hat believe me."

"That's as it may be," said the Inspector, "but I still have to consider your husband as a possible suspect until proven otherwise, I'm sorry, unless of course you have any information which might make me change my mind."

"Well for a start Inspector," said Jane who was clearly

upset about the Inspectors attitude, "my husband would no more consider shooting someone in the back with a shotgun than fly over the moon!"

"Forgive me for asking," said the Inspector, "but how on earth do you know how farmer Smith was killed, unless of course your husband told you how he did it."

Jane by now was getting even more upset and said, "obviously he didn't tell me because he wasn't there and as for how I know, you should by now have realised how quickly news gets round in a small community, I am right though, he was shot in the back with a shotgun wasn't he?"

"Yes, you are right," said the Inspector, "and I would be grateful if you would keep that information to yourself, there's obviously too many people who know already."

"Certainly," said Jane, "as you're new here Inspector I do have some information which may help with your investigation into the murder of farmer Smith, just to fill in a few gaps you might say."

"Thank you, Madam," said the inspector, "I'm sure any information you have will be of use to me."

"Can you tell me Inspector where you were based during the war," asked Jane.

"Is this relevant," said the inspector, "I was based in London for the entire duration of the war."

“Then you will obviously remember the Blitz on London, said Jane.

“I could hardly forget it,” replied the Inspector, “I doubt if anyone in London during the Blitz would be able to forget it.”

“Indeed Inspector, indeed,” said Jane, “then I shall tell you a story of those times, if you remember the Germans started with daylight raids but gradually we got better at getting our fighters up to intercept them and we shot more of their planes down and they changed to night time bombing.”

“Yes, I remember,” said the Inspector.

“My story concerns one of the earlier raids and started in the early hours of 15th September 1940, when a massive daylight raid took off from Germany together with Messerschmitt fighter planes for support and one of those planes was a Heinkel HE111 light bomber with a crew of five.”

“By this time in the war the Heinkel was becoming a little outdated and was very under armed, but just like our boys the crew of that bomber took off that morning to do their duty for their country.”

“I’m sorry,” said the Inspector, but I don’t see this has any bearing on the death of farmer Smith.”

“Bear with me Inspector,” replied Jane, “you will.”

"The Heinkel was an extremely noisy aircraft and was very unstable, if you lost concentration it would veer off to the side and had to be flown every inch of the way to England, it was not the sort of aircraft that you could relax at the controls whilst flying, it must have been exceptionally hard work on a mission lasting five hours or so."

"The crew had to work for their living too, the bombardier sat in the seat next to the pilot on the starboard side and had to duck under and forward to fire the machine gun or to use the bomb aimer, likewise the radio operator would also use a machine gun when under attack."

"On this particular morning the size of the raid was massive and we sent up our Spitfires and Hurricanes from Biggin Hill and the rest of 11 Sector to intercept them, you could see the dog fights from the ground, we attempted to take out the German fighters when they were on the way in, as they didn't have the fuel to stay to protect the bombers all the way but our chaps had time to get down, refuel and get back up to catch them on their way home ."

"I knew pilots from Biggin Hill who said the easiest time to take down the bombers was when they were leaving to go home as they didn't have their fighter escort, you could see planes coming down in flames and hope to God it wasn't one of ours, either way whichever side they were on it was someone's poor son who was inside."

"It must have been the same in London Inspector, whenever we had a plane crash into one of the fields all the young boys from the area would come out looking for souvenirs, bits of shrapnel or parts of the plane?"

"They did indeed Madam," said the Inspector, "it was our job as Police to stop it, it was after all illegal and in many cases dangerous, we found many a young lad walking home with a pocket full of live ammunition, I would imagine there are still old biscuit tins stashed under the beds of young boys containing bits of shrapnel and live rounds even now."

"Yes Inspector, I'm sure you're right," said Jane, "and if any of the crew was forced to bail out all the local farmers would be out to apprehend them if they were Germans, or to help if the poor chap was one of ours, either way the women folk took the silk parachute to make new knickers."

"Well, one of those poor souls was a Bombardier in one of those Heinkel's and he was in the front of the cockpit which was all glass, he was using his machine gun to defend his plane when they were hit by Ack-Ack guns causing the entire front of the plane to disintegrate, the explosive shells also knocked him out and when he came too he was floating down to earth on his parachute, I think God must have been with him that day."

"When he landed he was scared to death as he was surrounded by angry farmers with pitchforks and shotguns who were not at all pleased to see him, but luckily no harm came to him and he was arrested by the Police before being transported to the nearest prisoner of war camp at Crowhurst."

"I still don't see the point of this story Madam, if you don't mind me saying," said the Inspector.

"You will," said Jane, "a little more patience if you don't mind," she paused, "now, where was I?"

"Once processed at the camp and after some months they were segregated into the prisoners who could be trusted, those who were out and out Nazis who you would never be able to trust and those who we could usefully use to help in the community."

"This particular German Airman came to work here on Brightmoor Estate on the farms, eventually he became so trusted that he wasn't even taken back to camp every evening as they had done in the beginning, they let him lodge in the chauffeurs quarters, he was a very talented artist, in fact we have pictures of his in the house, we became very fond of him."

"Obviously Bob was too old for the war and had more important work to do here feeding the nation so was given Reserved Occupation status and he took the German Airman under his wing, so to speak and taught him everything he knew, I remember he used to say he'd never seen a man who had such a natural affinity with a horse, not only that but he could plough a furrow as straight as a die, quite a transformation from a man who was actually an artist."

"Later we had the assistance of the Land Army Girls who also surprised us with their ability but the German Airman passed on his knowledge to them and they worked as team, together they made a tremendous difference to the productivity of the estate during the war, in fact I think it safe to say without the help from the POW's and the Land Army we would be in a considerably worse state than we are in now."

"Towards the end of the war we got an American Fordson tractor but the German Airman never used it, in fact he hated it, Bob would often argue about the benefits of tractors against horses and that tractors were the way of the future but the German loved his horses too much to give them up."

"There was obviously some resentment from some of the locals what with him being German but after a while most of them realised he was on our side and what a difference he had made during the war, that German Airman's name was Herrmann Schmitt, the man everybody knows as farmer Henry Smith."

"I think Inspector," said Jane, "that my little story may help to put into perspective why I am so adamant that my husband Bob did not kill farmer Smith, there may be one or two in the village who still carry enough resentment to have done it but I very much doubt it and I suggest that you pop over the square to the Blue Boar or go round on market day and speak to the local farmers, I'm sure they will tell you the same thing."

Jane stood up and said, "Thank you for your time Inspector, I do hope should you hear of anything which might help in finding my husband you won't fail to notify me as soon as possible."

She left the room and was followed by Billy, James and Archie and when outside in the square James said, "I wouldn't mind a pint, how about you Archie?"

"Cracking idea," said Archie.

He turned and said to Jane, "If you don't mind, Archie and I will go for a quick pint in the Blue Boar, we might learn something from the locals, you never know, you and Billy go to the car, we will tell William you're ready to go and we can get a taxi back to Brightmoor later."

"Good idea," said Billy we will see you later for dinner.

James and Archie entered the pub which was a typical old country pub with oak beams, a low ceiling and a large fireplace which must have been very welcoming in the cold winter months, they could see William chatting with a couple of men at a table and when he saw them, he stood up downed his pint and said, "I assume they are ready to go home?"

"Yes," said James, "Archie and I are just going to have a quick pint and a little chat with the locals."

"Excellent Sir," said William, "I can come back for you gentlemen if you would like me to?"

"Yes please," said James, "if you could give us a couple of hours or so that would be splendid."

As William left, they went to the bar and Archie ordered two pints of bitter from the landlord who pulled the two pints and placed them on the bar. "You two must be the detectives from the big house, I suppose," said the landlord.

"Word certainly gets round quickly here doesn't it," said Archie.

"I suppose you'll be asking about poor old Herrmann," said the landlord.

"Herrmann?" questioned James.

"I always called him Hermann," said the landlord, that's how I knew him when I first met him when he was a Prisoner of War, I never got used to calling him Henry, he was a lovely man, he didn't deserve to die." He thought for a moment, "they had a row, they had a row the night Herrmann died, everyone in here saw it but I still don't believe Mr Trubshaw killed him."

"What exactly happened?" said James.

The landlord gestured to his barmaid to take over the bar and took James and Archie over to a quiet table in the corner of the pub.

They sat down and the landlord started, "well Sir, I remember it was raining that night, Mr Trubshaw had called a meeting as he wanted to speak to his tenant farmers about introducing the new British made Ferguson tractor, as I recollect he said they had an American tractor during the war on lend lease but he said he wanted to use British made tractors and that the modern way was going to be tractors and not horses."

"Herrmann was drinking quite heavily during the meeting and I could see he was getting more and more upset; we all knew how he felt about his horses and then finally he got up and shouted that he couldn't give up his horses grabbed his coat and hat and stormed out." "Mr Trubshaw ran after him and we could hear raised voices outside, then it seemed to quiet down and he came back in and finished the meeting."

"There was quite a heated discussion amongst the farmers who were still here, I don't remember what time Mr Trubshaw left, he must have sneaked out and left them to it and then the next day we heard the terrible news about Herrmann."

"Thank you very much," said James, "you've been most helpful," and he left with Archie and waited outside for

William to pick them up.

"Quick ciggie while we're waiting," asked James as he offered his silver cigarette case to Archie who took one and lit it, then offering the light to James.

James lit his cigarette and said, "lucky there's only two of us, never take the third light, you get your head blown off."

"Very true," said Archie.

It wasn't long before William pulled up in the car and they got in and sat in the pull-down seats nearest to the driver and wound down the glass partition separating themselves from William in the driving seat.

"Thank you for picking us up," said Archie.

"It's my pleasure Sir," said William

"Would you mind if I were to ask who were the two gentlemen you were talking to in the pub earlier," asked James.

"No Sir, not at all they were old Army chums of mine," said William, "we were all drivers together, I remember we all met at Woolwich when we were doing our basic training, those two were absolutely useless when they started but if you could manage to drive once round the parade ground you were in, they were always short of drivers, I taught them to drive properly, we'd sit on our beds and they would watch my feet and they would copy as I taught them how to double de-clutch, there were a lot less crunched changes when I'd finished with them."

"Are they local men," asked Archie.

"No Sir, they're both from South London, as far as I know they just came down here looking for work, what with so much of London being bombed they thought they might have better luck down here."

"I see," said James, "thank you for that William, by the way we have our associate Miss Cruickshank coming down on the morning train from London, would you be good enough to pick her up from the station please, she will be on the first train down, you shouldn't miss her, she's quite distinctive"

"Certainly Sir," said William as the car drew to a halt at the front door of Brightmoor and James and Archie got out.

James turned and said, "Goodnight William," and William replied, "Goodnight Sir."

ONE HELL OF A CHASE.

Archie and James were up early and before going down Archie popped his head into James's room to ask, "I must say I've rather got used to wearing tweed, should we stick with it."

"Certainly," said James, "we won't look out of place that way."

Billy was in the dining room getting his breakfast and he turned and said, "very smart chaps, you must be getting used to it Archie, very dapper again."

"Thank you," said Archie, "I must say I could get used to dressing in tweed, I bet it keeps the rain off."

"It certainly does, said Billy, "and keeps you warm in the winter, William tells me he's picking your Miss Cruickshank up from the station later."

"Yes, that's right," said James, "she's a very valuable asset to the firm and she's been doing some research for us so I look forward to what she may have found out."

They all filled their breakfast plates and sat down at the table and Billy commented, "Kedgeree again Archie, we'll make a countryman of you yet."

"You never know," said Archie.

"Actually," said James, "we're going to make an early start as we want to go to Folkstone harbour to have a look around the Blackbird boat."

"You'll need the cabin key," said Billy, "I'll get it for you before you leave, do you want William to drive you there."

"No thanks," said James, "I think I'll give the Bentley a bit of a blast."

"Have you sorted the route or would you like directions from William," asked Billy.

"My navigator Archie has it all under control, I'm sure, don't you Archie."

Yes indeed," said Archie, "South on the B2026, then A264 to Tonbridge Wells, A21 to Hawkhurst, then the A268 to Rye and I thought it would be fun to follow the A259 coast road to Folkstone."

“Sounds like you have it more than adequately under control Archie,” said Billy, “and while you’re away we shall entertain your Miss Cruickshank until your return.”

“Thank you, Billy,” said James, “that would be splendid, I just want to check the boat as you suggested there may be something fishy going on there.”

“What do you expect to find out at the boat,” asked Billy.

“To be honest Billy, I have no idea,” said James, “it’s just a feeling that we need to explore every avenue as to where your Uncle may be, or to find out what’s happened to him.”

“Would you like me to get William to bring your Bentley round to the front,” asked Billy.

“No thank you,” said James we’ll walk round and with that they got up from the breakfast table and went round to the garage.

As they walked the gravel was crunching under their feet and Archie said, “Do you have any idea what might have happened to their Uncle Bob?”

“Not yet Archie,” said James.

“Dare I ask if you think he’s dead? Said Archie.

James didn’t hesitate and replied, “I have to say I’m fairly certain that at the moment he is alive and well but the sooner we find him the better."

As they approached the garage, they could see that William had driven the Bentley outside the garage and had left it with the engine running.

"Morning gentlemen," he said, "I took the liberty of warming her up for you, it's a beautiful motor if you don't mind me saying Sir."

"Yes, I love her, I can't imagine ever getting rid of her," said James as he entered through the only door which was on the passenger side and slid across to the driver's seat followed by Archie to take his place as navigator in the passenger seat."

"Good luck, Sir," said William as they drove off throwing gravel up from the rear wheels, a legacy from still having a racing clutch fitted to the car.

It was a lovely warm day and James said, "smashing day for a drive," as he opened up the 4 ½ litre engine of the Bentley and with the advantage of the lack of traffic they were soon travelling at the usual breakneck speed that James liked to drive at.

The roads were clear and soon they were slowing down to drive through Tunbridge Wells and Archie commented, "There's some wonderful old buildings here, you can tell this town is posh."

"Yes, indeed," said James, "so posh its full name is Royal

Tonbridge Wells, it became fashionable as a Spa town when all the rich Londoners would come down to drink and to bathe in the spa waters, although having seen the water I find it hard to imagine it could have done any good."

"I think I'll stick to tap water for bathing and beer for drinking," said Archie and after consulting his map he said, "now we need to look out for the A21 to Hawkhust on the way out."

"I think you're probably right, beer for drinking," said James, and as they reached the outskirts of town, they turned off on the A21 and James let the car rip and soon they were on a very fast straight piece of road where he was about to really gun it but saw in the distance a horse and cart laden with milk churns.

"Shame," said James, "we really could have given the old girl a good blast down here but you don't want to scare the horses."

They slowed down as quietly and gently as they could and crept past the cart, the farmer driving the cart gave a wave to acknowledge them and to thank them for slowing down.

It wasn't long before they were finally on the coast road to Folkstone, "I don't know what it is about the sea that is so fascinating," said James, "it must have something to do with living on an island."

The rest of the journey to Folkstone was taken at a more leisurely pace as they took time to admire the view, "it's wonderful to look out at the sea and not worry about an invasion from the other side," said Archie, as they finally parked up in the square near the harbour.

"Right, let's go and find this boat," said James.

"It shouldn't be hard to spot it," said Archie, "from the way they describe it, I imagine it must be a bit of a gin palace and rather splendid."

As they walked down to the harbour they could see Blackbird moored on the opposite side of the harbour and what a magnificent boat it was and much larger than they had expected, stunning white paintwork combined with the dark teak wood of the decks and the contrasting oak of the upper cabin, the brass fitments on deck glistening in the sunlight.

"That's quite a boat," said James.

As they got closer, they could see two men on deck with a crowbar attempting to open the rear doors of the cabin but as they were made of a fairly substantial piece of oak, they were having little luck.

Archie called out, "stop that you buggers," which caused the men to drop the crowbar and jump off the boat onto the quayside and run off towards some fishermen's huts which were near the beach, he started running after them and called back to James, “fetch the car and follow when you can,” he remembered that James still carried damage to his knee from the raid at St Nazaire during the war.

As Archie shot off round the corner, James went back to fetch the Bentley which fired up on the button, however in the meantime Archie was being led a merry dance round the fishermen’s huts and having to jump over crab pots and nets which were being thrown at him by the fleeing men.

When he was beginning to catch them he saw the men dart to their left between the huts with the obvious intention to make their way back to the road, he put a spurt on and turned the corner and stopped in his tracks as he faced one of the men, when from behind the other cracked him round the back of the head with a fairly hefty piece of wood, causing him to collapse unconscious to the ground.

He regained consciousness some minutes later and realised James was calling for him and called back somewhat groggily, “I’m over here,” he said, “the buggers knocked me out.”

“How are you,” asked James, “are you up to continuing?”

“Well I’m seeing double and I’ve a splitting headache but besides that I’m fine,” said Archie, “let’s go and get ‘em.”

As they made their way to the car which James had parked in the road he said, "I think we can still catch them, this is the coast road, they didn't come back past me so they can only have gone in the other direction towards Dover."

They jumped aboard the Bentley and Archie took out his handkerchief and held it to a small cut on the back of his head as James dropped the clutch on the Bentley leaving black tyre marks on the road from the spinning rear wheels.

James drove like a man possessed causing Archie to comment, "I can see how you won so many races."

"An awful lot of it is down to the car," said James, as he opposite locked his way round yet another corner, "I'm glad I didn't have a blower fitted, W O was not at all keen on them, I always thought that with the heavy supercharger mounted out front it made the car understeer too much," and as if to prove his point he was virtually sideways at the next bend.

When the road straightened out for a brief moment Archie called out, "I saw a car in the distance just then, I'm bloody sure I saw a car."

"We're going to catch them now Archie old man," said James, "there's a hefty tyre lever stashed behind your seat if you want to grab it you can repay the favour with regard to your head!"

"Damn good idea," said Archie, as they drew ever closer to the car up the road which looked like a rather second-hand old Austin.

"Blast," said James, "they've spotted us."

The driver of the Austin picked up speed and became more and more erratic brushing the hedgerow as he went round each corner and then finally causing blue smoke to come out of the exhaust pipe.

"We've got him now," said James, but unfortunately in the distance they could see a hay cart pulling out from a field which caused James to slow down immediately, however the Austin kept going and shot past the cart, smoke still bellowing from its exhaust.

Not surprisingly the horse reared up in fright and deposited all the hay bales in the road causing James to stop as the road was blocked and to help the farmer calm his horse and to assist in putting all the bales back on the cart.

Having seen the farmer on his way James and Archie decided there was obviously no point in trying to continue the chase so backed the Bentley into the field and turned round and headed for home.

"We may not have caught them," said James, "but at least we have proved there is something fishy going on connected with the boat, we'll stop on the way back and check it's secure and then go back to Brightmoor."

As they pulled up at the harbour, they could see a fishing boat had come in and moored behind the Blackbird, with what appeared to be a Captain and a couple of fishermen who were on board stashing the gear and mending the nets.

"Hello chaps," said James, "good catch today?"

"Not bad Sir," said the Captain, "could always be better."

"Yes, of course," said James, "I wonder if I might ask you a few questions, I assume this is your home port?"

"Yes Sir," replied the Captain, "I suppose you're interested in the Blackbird; I'm guessing you're not here to buy some fish."

"Well, now you mention it, both would be good," replied James, "but first I was wondering if you could tell us if you've seen any strange goings on recently, any odd-looking characters hanging about, that sort of thing?"

"There were two men just this week hanging around but I heard they were just down from London looking for work, as for Blackbird she hasn't been out recently which is a bit strange as Mr Trubshaw used to go over to France for the weekend every couple of weeks or so, they usually go over on Friday have a bit of a party and come back on Monday," said the Captain.

James thanked the Captain and bought five fillets of cod and headed back to Brightmoor and said, “fresh cod for dinner should be good don’t you think Archie?”

“I wonder if we can get the cook to rustle up some chips too,” replied Archie, “with plenty of salt and vinegar.”

“I don’t know about the salt and vinegar,” said James but the fish and chips sounds good, I’ll ask when we get back.”

Having parked the Bentley in the garage, they were walking back to the house when they saw Jane at the window of the drawing room, she waved to them and opened the French Doors for them to come in and said, “ I know it may sound silly but I was reminded of it when I heard you both walking on the gravel outside, I keep thinking I can see Bob, I hear the crunch of the gravel and look out but he always seems to have disappeared, I’m afraid I’m going a little do-lally.”

“I wouldn’t worry about it too much Jane,” said James, “you must be under a considerable amount of strain at the moment, it’s not surprising your mind is playing tricks with you.”

“I’m afraid Archie took a bit of a crack to the back of his head today, nothing too serious but I wonder if we could get it cleaned up,” asked James.

“Certainly, just go and wait in the study, I’ll get my lady’s maid to come with some iodine and some cotton wool," said Jane.

"By the way," said James, "I hope you don't think us rude but we had the opportunity to buy some fresh fish while we were at Folkstone and Archie was wondering if cook might knock up some fish and chips for us all for dinner, he'd be even more delighted if she had some salt and vinegar for him too."

"I'll pop off and see cook straight away I'm sure that would be possible, I assume he'd like it battered as one might get in a chippy," she giggled, "oh, by the way your associate Miss Cruickshank has arrived she's in the dining room with Billy if you'd like to see them, I'll come and find you after I've spoken to cook and my maid."

Archie went and waited in the study while James made his way to the dining room and on entering, he said, "hello, Billy and hello, Miss Cruickshank, how very nice to see you again, I trust you had a good journey down."

"Yes, thank you Sir," she replied, "thank you for the ticket, I don't usually travel first class."

"My pleasure," said James, "only the best for our Miss Cruickshank."

"I hear you've had quite a day by all accounts," said Billy, "we've been chatting here after luncheon, perhaps we should go and sit more comfortably in the drawing room?"

James responded positively and they made their way to the drawing room and sat down on two long sofas which were placed either side of the fireplace facing each other, James on one side and Billy and Miss Cruickshank the other.

"How on Earth do you know what sort of day we've had," asked James, as Billy replied immediately, "I would have thought you had become used to the countryside jungle telephone by now James."

"Yes, of course," said James, "I was forgetting that."

Just then Archie entered the drawing room and said hello to them all and Billy asked, "how's your head?"

"Not too bad thanks to Florence Nightingale, she was very gentle" said Archie, "I've got a bit of a lump but the cut is quite small, so a dab of iodine seems to have done the trick."

"That's good to know, I hear you purchased some fish whilst you were on your travels," said Billy, "and we are to experience the delights of a fish and chip supper for dinner tonight."

Archie smiled, "I'm rather hoping so, yes."

"Then I suggest we all have a quick wash and brush up and change for dinner," said Billy, "after you Miss Cruickshank."

They all left the drawing room and went upstairs to

change for dinner and as they went up the stairs Archie said, "the jungle telephone business is quite a thing down here in the country, they seem to know everything, I wonder if they know who's going to win the two thirty at Epsom tomorrow."

"I wouldn't be surprised if they do know," said James as he went into his room, "see you downstairs Miss Cruickshank," she nodded and went off to her room.

After washing and changing, James and Archie met Billy on the stairs coming down and went into the dining room together and sat down and were served with some red wine from the footman. "This is rather splendid," said James, "I wouldn't mind a few bottles of this myself."

"Actually, this is the stuff that Uncle Bob brings back from Calais whenever he pops over for a weekend jolly up in Blackbird," said Billy.

"Well, when this is over and we've found Uncle Bob," said James, "you can put me down for a case or two."

The doors of the dining room opened and Aunt Jane entered looking as immaculate as ever, closely followed by Miss Cruickshank who was wearing a strapless taffeta cocktail dress in a rather stunning tangerine yellow, the effect of the dress and Miss Cruickshank's ample bosom was not lost on Archie, who whispered, "I say!"

"Good evening Miss Cruickshank," said Aunt Jane, "you look positively wonderful, my dear that colour really suits you, do come and sit next to me."

Miss Cruickshank walked over and sat down next to Aunt Jane who said, "do tell me your name, I can't keep calling you Miss Cruickshank."

"Thank you, Madam," said Miss Cruickshank, "my name is Amelia."

"What a wonderful name," said Aunt Jane pausing, "Amelia, my dear you simply must call me Jane, I'm sure we we're going to be the best of friends, perhaps having all gone through a war together it's time to loosen some of the more stuffy protocols of yesteryear." "Do please tell me about yourself and how you came to be working with James and Archie?"

"Amelia regaled Jane with her full life story, from her humble beginning as a Vicar's daughter to her time as a nude dancer at the Windmill Theatre and finally to her eventual arrival working for the Arbuthnott and Cluff Detective Agency."

"Well," said Jane when she had finished, "my dear Amelia, you seem to have loosened quite a few of the stuffy protocols already."

"What a fascinating story," said Billy, "now James, besides Archie's crack on the head, how did your day go?"

"It was a bit of a Curate's egg really, it started quite well, we had a cracking drive down to Folkstone but it went a little downhill after that," said James.

"At least we saw off the couple of scallywags who were attempting to break into the Blackbird boat, although unfortunately we were unable to catch them and we still have no idea why they were breaking in, I assume there is nothing of significant value left on the boat?"

"Not really," said Billy, "most of the fitting are bolted down in case of rough sea and who'd want to steal a chair or a table anyway."

"Yes, it seems strange to me," said James, "it's lucky we just happened to arrive at the right time."

"I think it might have been better had we arrived a little earlier," said Archie, "then it might have been me creeping up on them and giving them a crack across the back of the head, instead of the other way round."

The doors to the dining room opened and Wilson the Butler entered followed by four footmen each carrying a tray with a folded newspaper on it which they placed on the plates in front of each of the dinner guests, he said, "I believe this is as you requested Madam?"

Jane opened her package to reveal the battered fish and chips and said, "Excellent, thank you Wilson that will do nicely."

"Very good, Madam," said Wilson, "the salt and vinegar is on the table, if that will be all?"

"Yes Wilson," said Jane.

"Splendid," said Wilson, "tickety-boo," and left the dining room.

"How's that for you Archie," said Jane with a smile on her face.

"Just what the doctor ordered," said Archie as he tucked into the beautiful white fish and splendid chips made from local potatoes.

When dinner was finished, they all returned to the drawing room for drinks, the men having whiskey and soda and the women plumping for gin and tonic, they all sat down in front of the fireplace again, the three men facing the two women.

"So, what do you have in store for tomorrow James," said Jane.

"Well I'd certainly like to catch the buggers that gave me this bump on the back of my head," said Archie.

"Yes indeed," said James, "but first I'd like to get Amelia to do some more research for me, I wonder if she might have use of a telephone for the day."

"Certainly," said Jane, "Amelia my dear, there is the Pink Room which is my private room just up the corridor, it has its own telephone line and you're welcome to use it as and when you need to."

"Thank you, Jane," said Amelia, "you're very kind."

"It's the least I could do, anything which might help to find Bob," said Jane as she got up to get herself another drink but as she walked closer to the window, she suddenly dropped her glass and called out, "Bob!"

Amelia went over and picked up the glass from the carpet, got a fresh glass and made her another gin and tonic and said, "here drink this, I'm not sure if gin is good for shock but I see no reason to think it will do any harm, come and sit down with me."

"I'm sorry Jane," said James, "but I'm sure it wasn't Bob it was just a trick of the light on the windowpane and it's getting late I suspect you're getting a little tired, perhaps you should be going to bed, would you like Amelia to take you up?"

"Yes," said Jane "I think I am getting a little tired, perhaps a good night's sleep will help."

"I'm sure it will," said Amelia as she finished her drink and got up and escorted Jane up to her bedroom, "Goodnight all," she said as she went out of the door.

When they had left the room, Billy said, "I'm rather worried about Aunt Jane I afraid she will make herself ill, she worries far too much."

"Unfortunately it's not that easy to fix," said Archie, "I remember during the Blitz women would go to the doctors as they were having trouble with their nerves and the Doctor would hand them a box of five Weights cigarettes and a box of matches with the advice to pull themselves together!"

"I very much doubt it would have helped," said Billy.

"I'm sure it didn't make a ha'peth of difference," said Archie.

"Perhaps we can ask Amelia to keep an eye on her, it might be a good idea if we ask Jane to help Amelia tomorrow, it will give her something to take her mind off things for a while," said James.

"Good idea," said Archie.

"Do you have a plan for tomorrow James," asked Billy.

" I must admit I don't have a set plan but I would dearly love to find out where the scallywags from today are hiding, I'm rather hoping we might get some help from the local jungle telephone, I shall call in at the Police Station for a start, someone must have seen something, "said James.

"Perhaps an early night might be in order so we're fresh in the morning," said Billy as he escorted James and Archie upstairs to their rooms.

They all said goodnight and as Archie was just about to

enter his room he turned to James and said, "I know we didn't catch them, but it was one hell of a chase."

"Yes," said James, "one hell of a chase."

IF YOU GO DOWN TO THE WOODS TODAY.

James and Archie had taken breakfast early and were just leaving the dining room when Miss Cruickshank came down the stairs.

"Good morning Amelia," said James, "and how are we today?"

"I'm very well Sir," she said, "but I'm still a little worried about Jane, she was quite upset when I took her to her bedroom last night, I went in to see if I could put her mind at rest but she's still insistent that she's seeing Bob."

"Well, I suppose it's only to be expected," said James, "try and keep her mind off it today if you can, you can share the workload, I know you're doing fairly well with regard to Lord Eddleton's relatives, perhaps you can ask her to look into what happened to the owner of Whintons after Uncle Bob bought the firm, we still don't know yet why Bob has gone into hiding, let's see if together you can rake something up."

"I'll do my best Sir," said Miss Cruickshank, "what are you two up to this morning?"

"We're off to the woods today," said Archie, "we just had a call from Inspector Andrews."

"Well look out for the teddy bears, especially if they're having a picnic," said Miss Cruickshank.

"We will indeed," said James smiling, as he and Archie left the house to pick up the Bentley.

When they arrived at the Police Station they went straight in and up to the desk where Sergeant Collins said, "good morning gentlemen, Inspector Andrews is expecting you, he asked that you see him as soon as you arrive, just down the corridor I'm sure you remember the way."

"Yes Sergeant," said James as he led Archie down the corridor and knocked on Inspector Andrews door.

"Come in," said Inspector Andrews, "take a seat if you like."

There was still only one chair so they declined and both stood and James said, "well Inspector what can we do for you today?"

"Word has got round about your exploits of yesterday, shame you didn't catch them," said the Inspector, and turning to Archie asked, "how's your head Sir by the way?"

"Not too bad," said Archie, "I've a bit of a lump but other than that I'm fine, thanks for asking."

"I imagine you might be able to identify the men who attacked you," asked the Inspector.

"I'm sure we can Inspector," said James, "but Archie got a closer look at one of them, unfortunately just before the other clumped him on the head."

"Excellent," said the Inspector, "we had a tip off this morning that they are hiding in Oakdown Wood, so if you'd like to come with us, we will go and apprehend the thugs."

"I look forward to that," said Archie, "I can't wait to see them get their just deserts, let's go."

"Obviously it will be the Police who will be arresting these thugs," said the Inspector, "we don't want anyone taking the law into their own hands, do we Sir."

"Yes of course," said Archie, "after all we would hate it if either of these fellows should accidentally fall upon my fist."

"Indeed Sir," said the Inspector, "we wouldn't want you damaging your fist, would we," and with that he led them out of the office to the square outside where there were two Police cars complete with a full complement of Constables waiting. "Perhaps you two gentlemen would like to follow behind in your own car, if you wouldn't mind."

James and Archie fired up the Bentley and formed up behind the waiting Police cars and followed on as they drove off towards Oakdown Woods which were some three miles away and as they got closer the Police slowed down and came to a halt at a lane which led up to the woods, from where a small plume of smoke could be seen rising.

The Inspector got out of the leading car and said, "we don't want them getting away this time, so I was wondering, as you gentlemen have some experience with this sort of action from your time in the Army perhaps you two could go and sneak round the back to cover their retreat as it were."

"It would be a pleasure Inspector, "said Archie, "just one thing though, we weren't in the Army, we were in the Commandos, there's a great deal of difference."

The Inspector looked at Archie quizzically and said "I'll give you ten minutes for you to get into position before we come up the lane full pelt."

"That should be more than enough time for us, although from the look of the smoke it seems a shame to interrupt their breakfast" said James as he and Archie crept off round the back of the wood.

The Inspector was looking as his watch and standing by the door of the Police car as he counted down, "three, two, one, go!" and jumping in the car waved the others to follow ringing their bells as they went.

Both cars skidded to a halt and all eight of the Policemen jumped out and rushed into the woods where the smoke was coming from only to be faced with two men on the ground trussed up like chickens with the guide rope from the tent which they had been using.

James and Archie were standing over them and in unison said, "hello Inspector, what kept you!"

"How the devil did you manage that," said the Inspector.

"Commandos," said Archie.

"Well, that's as it may be," said the Inspector, "I shall now be taking these men into custody and reading them the riot act, perhaps you two chaps could come for identification purposes, if you wouldn't mind."

"Certainly Inspector," said James.

When they were driving back to the Police Station James turned to Archie and said, "just as well they never fell onto your fist, the Inspector would have been upset."

"Yes," said Archie, "although how on earth he ran into that heavy frying pan I'll never know."

When they arrived back at the Police Station, they were directed into the Interview room by Constable Lamb and found the Inspector and Sergeant Collins seated at a table and the two thugs seated opposite them, both were wearing what looked to be demob suits, and one of the men appeared to have a black eye.

"Now, gentlemen I don't want either of you to waste my time," said the Inspector, "I want your names and I want to know if either of you has a criminal record and before you answer don't forget we have files and fingerprints so we will be double checking."

Both men appeared to be in their twenties although one was slightly older and it was he who started, "my name's John Spearman and my friend is Chris Brown, neither of us have a criminal record, we've not long ago been demobbed, I'm sorry we're just unemployed Army Servicemen looking for some work."

The Sergeant who was taking notes said, "I can tell from your accent that you both come from London, what part exactly?"

The younger man looked a little like a rabbit caught in headlights said, "my name's Chris Brown," he paused, "my names Christopher, and we both come from Peckham, I'm so sorry Sir, we're not bad people, we were only doing what we were paid to do."

"And what exactly," said the Inspector, "were you paid to do?"

"I know this is going to sound ridiculous Sir," said Christopher, "but we were going to be paid to repossess the Blackbird boat."

"Why would you be doing that Christopher?" asked the Inspector, "and who indeed was going pay you to do so."

"I don't suppose there's any chance of a fag," said John, "I'm dying for a smoke."

James took out a packet of Senior Service and a box of matches and tossed them onto the table, where both the young lads took one each and lit them up.

"Feeling better now lads," asked James.

"Yes, thank you," said John, as his friend Christopher continued, "we were told we were to take the boat back as it was a bad gambling debt and I have no idea who we were working for it was just some chap we met in a pub in Covent Garden."

"So, what exactly do you know about boats," said James, "you said you were in the Army."

"To be honest Sir," said Christopher, "we know absolutely bugger all about boats but we needed a job so we told the fellow we were in the Navy and he believed us."

"You're telling us, you met a man in a pub in London and you have absolutely no idea who he was," said James, "and then you told him you were in the Navy, when you don't know the first thing about boats and then he asked you both to steal a boat for him and you two were then stupid enough to try to do it."

"Yes Sir," said Christopher, "that's pretty much it."

"All I can say," said James, "it's lucky we came along when we did, Lord only knows where you two would have ended up had you managed to break in and actually start the ruddy thing, I would have thought they'd have been trying to rescue you from the ruddy Atlantic!" "Where exactly where you supposed to take the boat should you have actually managed to steal the thing?"

"Well Sir, we were supposed to take the boat to Dover and wait and someone would come and take the boat from us and pay us, it all seemed so easy"

"You do realise there are still plenty of mines along the coast," said James, "and why on earth did they pick Dover, one of the busiest ports on the South coast of England, Lord knows how you chaps would have navigated your way into Dover especially as it would have been dark by the time you got there!"

"Well Sir, they said, the best place to hide a boat is in amongst a harbour which is filled with boats, in plain sight they said and as for our ability to navigate, I have to say that we did rather embellish our Naval experience, if we'd have been half as good as we said we were it would have been a piece of cake," said Christopher, "Knowing what you've just told me, I have to say I'm very glad we failed, we'd have probably blow ourselves to pieces."

"I know it may sound as if we're making it up but you can check what we're saying quite easily," said Christopher, "we met in the Nags Head pub in James Street, Covent Garden which is close to The Royal Opera House, it was turned into a Mecca Ballroom during the war, we used to go there looking for girls whenever we had any leave, we're not making it up, honest."

"I'm taking notes here," said Sergeant Collins, "all I can say is this nonsense has got to be the truth, it's too ridiculous for them to be making it up!"

"Yes, thank you Sergeant," said the Inspector, "so how much were you going to be paid then Sonny Jim," said the Inspector who was beginning to get a little tired of what seemed to him like a completely made up story.

"Nothing," said Christopher.

"Nothing," repeated the Inspector, "do you think I was born yesterday?"

"It's true Inspector," said Christopher, "he gave us the car which we would have been pleased with on its own had it not turned out to be a load of rubbish but we were promised a percentage of the value of the boat when we handed it over, although they didn't say what percentage."

James stood up and started slowly pacing the room, "I'm afraid Inspector that these two Herbert's are actually telling the truth, The Royal Opera House is close to the Nags Head Pub in James Street and it was turned into a Mecca Ballroom during the war, I've been there myself, so perhaps if this is true then maybe the rest is too and we have just come across two of the most inept criminals you've ever had the pleasure of arresting!"

"That's it," said the Inspector, "I've had enough of this, John Spearman and Christopher Brown I'm arresting you both for the attempted breaking and entering on the Blackbird boat and assault on Mr Archibald Cluff and for," he paused as he was trying to think of something else he could legally arrest them for, "and for wasting Police time and for confusing and annoying me, take them to the cells Sergeant."

As they were about to leave the interview room the Inspector turned to James and Archie and said, "I can't believe the only thing we've got on those two is attempted breaking and entering and assault."

"Perhaps it might be worth sending some of your men to their camp in the woods and to bring back their stuff and go through it with a fine tooth comb," said James, "I suspect there will be little of any use but it's worth a try, the car may be registered to someone, if you'd be kind enough to let us know should you turn anything up I would be grateful."

"Before you take us away I'd like to say something," said John, "we're sorry Sir, we're very sorry, we're not bad people Chris and I, we just wanted a chance, a chance for a better life, they said that after the first War didn't they, a land fit for heroes, well that's what we were trying to get."

"Do you remember what it was like on VE Day, we were lucky enough to be on leave that day, the 8th May 1945, we'd heard Richard Dimbleby on the wireless the day before telling us that the Germans had unconditionally surrendered at Reims in France, we knew Hitler was dead, all we had to do now was finish of the Japs and the whole thing would be over, it was just a matter of time."

"Chris and I went up to Town that day and on the way, we passed street parties with trestle tables and chairs stretched along the middle of the road, Union flags hanging up everywhere, bunting strung from one side of the street to the other the entire neighbourhood was taking part, there was joy in the air."

"The Church bells were ringing out, we hadn't heard Church bells for years, there were parades with local dignitaries, boy scouts, girl guides and children in fancy dress, there was a carnival atmosphere, in some streets they had dragged a piano out from one of the houses and were gathered round singing."

"The whole world seemed to have gone up Town that day, there were hundreds of thousands of people who were singing and dancing and when we got to Trafalgar Square people were paddling in the fountains, the feeling of elation was electric, I kissed more girls that day than I had done in my whole life up until then."

"Every Londoner knew they were safe at last, safe from the bombs, the doodle bugs, the V1's and V2's, no longer would you go to bed at night wondering if you'd be alive in the morning."

"People had come up to Town from all over the country and when you spoke to most of them they said how surprised they were at the amount of bomb damage the city had seen, I suppose Chris and I had become used to it in a way, every leave we got when we came home, there were more and more homes and buildings gone and no doubt more people gone along with them, some of them you knew, plenty you didn't but it was a price we had to pay to beat the Germans and win the war."

"During the day we made our way up to St Pauls and were amazed at the amount of damaged buildings around it, but it was a ruddy miracle it survived at all, my mum kept a copy of The Daily Mail and I remember the picture on the front page of St Pauls engulfed by fire, I think it was in the winter of 1940 when the Blitz was still on, mum wanted to save the copy but we had no toilet paper so it was cut into squares for a better purpose."

A tear welled up in Chris's eye, who interrupted John's story to say, "I loved your mum, she was like a mother to me, I was an orphan and she took me in and treated me like family, I miss her and dad so much."

"You are family," said John, "I miss them terribly too, it's ironic the way they died, dad had spent days digging up the back garden and building an Anderson shelter, he dug it deep and covered it with tons of earth, he made a right proper job of it but mum would never use it, she said she was claustrophobic, it was too closed in for her so they used to sleep under the dining room table for years, although with no sides I can't see it would have been much protection."

"Then one night there was a bomb further down the street which blew all the windows in at of the front of the house, it put the wind up mum good and proper, so the next night mum said she'd have a go at sleeping in the Anderson which they did but later that night the shelter caught a direct hit, it took half the street out as well, ruddy Hitler!"

"We understood how people were feeling on VE Day, in a way we'd been through it too and as we made our way down to Buckingham Palace there were loud speakers which had been put up so the crowds could listen to Mr Churchill's speech at three o'clock, he said this was our hour, it was a victory of the great British nation as a whole and how we had been left to fight Hitler alone and we had for a whole year and how we'd now triumphed." "John continued with an impersonation of Churchill, "We may allow ourselves a brief period of rejoicing, today is Victory in Europe Day."

"There was a fly past over the Palace which some said was bringing troops home, I don't know if it was true but we knew from reports on the wireless that they had opened up the prison camps and had been releasing our troops two days before, it certainly was a sight, all them planes"

"People went barmy, some climbed lampposts and sat on the top, I couldn't much see the point of that though, as all you can do when you get to the top is come down again, but everyone was doing daft things, some climbed onto the roof of the passing taxis and even attempted to dance whilst up there, luckily it was too crowded for the taxi to reach any significant speed, I expect someone would have caught them if they had fallen off though."

"King George VI broadcast a message from Buckingham Palace over the speakers and then the King and Queen came out on the balcony with the young Princesses Margret and Elizabeth who was in her ATS Uniform to wave to the crowd, a massive cheer went up, it seemed like everyone was waving a Union flag, they came out several times during the day and finally at five o'clock they came out again, although this time Mr Churchill was with them, what a sight for sore eyes!"

"Big Ben even rang out during the day, another sound we hadn't heard for some time," he paused for a moment, "it was also a time of sadness as little things during the day would remind you of mum and dad and others we had lost but then suddenly a girl would come up and kiss you for no reason and you'd be happy again."

"We'd still had blackouts at night even up until that day and as the evening went on and it became darker and darker Buckingham Palace was lit up by floodlights, we could hardly believe it, floodlights of all things and the Royal Family came out for the last time at ten o'clock, it was like a fairground there were lights everywhere, The Houses of Parliament, St Pauls, Piccadilly Circus and all over the place."

"We made our way slowly back to Trafalgar Square which was lit up like a Christmas tree, there was a placard round the bottom of Nelson's Column declaring Victory over Germany 1945 and people were dancing and celebrating well into the early hours of the morning, someone started a conga line which went completely round the square."

"It was getting on for three or four in the morning when we made our way back to our digs in Peckham and as we walked along it was so strange to see the curtains open in people's houses with light flooding out into the street, you could also see the glow in the distance where people had lit bonfires, no bombers tonight."

"I know we've done wrong and we'll have to pay the price for that but I think our worst crime is being so stupid, I can tell you Inspector that Chris and I both feel proper Charley's for being taken in so easily but we were just looking for some of the optimistic feeling we experienced on VE Day and we thought this job was it, hopefully we will have learned our lesson from this experience and won't get duped so easily next time."

"Well that was a very moving little speech there," said the Inspector, "but I'm afraid the law is the law and I still have to arrest you both, Sergeant would you take these men to the cells."

The Sergeant stood up and escorted the men from the room and as they were leaving the Inspector said, "make sure they have some supper, after all they missed their breakfast this morning."

James and Archie left the Police Station, they boarded the Bentley and headed back to Brightmoor and by the time they had parked the car they could see the others going in for dinner and came straight in to join them.

Billy stood up and said, "hello chaps, had a good day?"

"Interesting," said Archie as they sat down and ate their

dinner.

“We caught the two chaps who were trying to steal the Blackbird,” said James, “and it turns out they were not the major criminals we were expecting, more like Laurel and Hardy I’m afraid, just two rather naïve young men hoping to make a better future for themselves, I must say I feel rather sorry for them.”

“Unfortunately we don’t yet know who employed them to try to steal the boat but I’m sure we’ll find out in the fullness of time, I’m just hoping that the fellows who employed them are as inept as our two robbers, they bluffed their way into getting the job by saying they had been in the Navy since the beginning of the war, which is almost true except they were in the Army and not the Navy.”

“They also told them they were experienced sailors who could handle anything, which I think can safely be described as a load of rowlocks, whereas the truth of the matter is, I doubt if their sailing experience is much more than a quick row around Regents Park boating lake and a rather more dangerous trip on a landing craft to the Normandy beaches on D Day.”

“To tell the truth it’s very lucky we stopped them getting away with Blackbird or there is every chance they would have drifted away into the Atlantic Ocean or blown themselves and the boat up in the nearest uncleared naval minefield.”

"I must say I feel a little sorry for them," said Billy, after all they did their bit for King and Country and now, they've made a very foolish mistake, it seems such a shame, have they been charged with anything yet?"

"So far," said James, "it's attempted breaking and entering and assault on Archie, although if the Inspector had his way, I think he'd like to add more charges, we did suggest treason but he didn't see the funny side of it."

"One imagines," said Billy, "that if you and Archie had a sudden change of mind and became somewhat confused and were unable to identify these chaps there is every chance they might not even be charged and would be able to walk from the Police Station tomorrow as free men without a stain on their characters."

"Yes indeed," said James, "I see what you mean."

"Amelia and I have had a fairy constructive day too," said Jane.

"Yes we have," said Amelia, "I have done some fairly extensive research on Lord Eddleton and his surviving relatives and am expecting a telegram tomorrow when I will have the full picture but I've drawn a bit of a blank with anything relating to Whintons Engineering perhaps you might have better luck with a trip to the works?"

"Excellent idea, Amelia," said James as he finished his dinner and continued, "well, it's been a long day, it seems we have all been busy, I suggest a quick nightcap and then to bed for an early start tomorrow."

BROOKLANDS.

"Morning all," said Amelia as she entered the dining room where James, Archie and Billy were just finishing breakfast.

"You're up bright and early," she said.

"Yes," said Billy, "we've a busy day planned for today and I'm going to take the chaps in my new Mk VI, it needs some more gentle driving to run her in properly."

"What are your plans for the day Amelia," asked James.

"Well, Jane is taking me for a little run out in her MG which should be fun, I think she's feeling a little better, she's not quite so worried about Bob as she was, helping me with the research gave her something else to occupy her mind, perhaps we can find a tea room and have a cream tea."

"I'm so glad to hear that," said James, as Jane entered the dining room looking stunning as usual in an extremely vibrant A line frock with multi coloured floral print.

As she sat down Amelia said, "what a wonderful frock, is it new."

"Yes, I've just had it made, it's the very latest style from Paris," said Jane, "I've been saving my coupons for some time for this amount of material but I think the new look is worth it."

"It certainly is," said Amelia, "it's beautiful."

"I hear you two are off for a drive," said Billy, "I hope you have a lovely day," and with that Archie, Billy and James got up from the table and made their way to the front door where Billy's new Bentley was waiting for them.

Billy opened the suicide front door and sat in the driver's seat, James joined him in the front while Archie sat in the back and James said, "there's nothing like the smell of a new car, is there, the wood, the distinctive smell of the new leather and the smell of the engine as she warms up, beautiful."

"Yes, you're right James," said Billy, "I love the smell of new leather."

Archie sat back in the seat as the car gently glided along

and felt like he was being chauffeured, "I could get used to this," he thought.

"No racing about today James, I'm afraid," said Billy, "what with one thing and another and Bob's disappearance I haven't had time to run her in yet, it will be a nice leisurely drive today."

As they arrived outside the Police Station, Billy slowed and gently stopped by a young boy who was standing by the kerbside, "lovely car Sir," he said, "would you like me to keep an eye on it for you while you're away."

Billy smiled as they got out of the car and he took a bright new thruppenny bit from his pocket and gave it to the young lad, saying, "take good care of her, young fellow."

The young boy was delighted with the bright new coin and said, "I will Sir, thank you."

As they entered the Police Station Sergeant Collins said, "good morning Sir, the Inspector knows you're coming, I'm sure you can find your own way to his office by now."

"Yes, we can, thank you Sergeant," said James as he led the way to the Inspectors office.

They all stood up when they were inside and Billy said, "good morning Inspector, we need to have a quick chat about the fellows you apprehended yesterday, it seems that having thought about it James and Archie are both of the opinion that they were not close enough to the two young chaps to categorically say they were the men trying to break into Blackbird."

"Pardon," said the Inspector somewhat surprised, "you've changed your minds gentlemen?"

"Yes, we have," said Archie.

The Inspector stuttered, "well, what about the assault charge, don't tell me you've forgotten they attacked you Sir, if you don't mind me asking?"

"I don't see how a charge of assault is possible Inspector," said Archie, "as I seem to have forgotten completely what the two fellows looked like, I only had a very brief look at one of them before I was hit from behind."

"And I wouldn't be pressing any charges, even if we could identify the culprits," said Billy, "so I would respectfully request the release of the two young men, thank you Inspector."

"This is most irregular," said the Inspector as he led the way to the front desk, "Sergeant, release Spearman and Brown will you."

A few moments later they arrived at the front desk looking slightly dishevelled and somewhat confused, the Sergeant asked them to sign their release papers and said, "alright lads, you're free to go."

"You're coming with us," said Billy as he led them to the waiting car, he thanked the young lad for his diligent work guarding it and opened the rear door for Archie, John and Christopher and jumped in the front with James.

Billy started the car and said, "right, we're having a day trip to Brooklands, the home of British motorsport as they used to say."

"I don't understand," said Chris, "why are we free?"

"Well," said Billy, "James, Archie and myself had a discussion and we came to the conclusion that the only crime you two had committed was to be a pair of complete idiots and we think a night in the cells is a long enough sentence for that."

"I think it safe to say we're evens too," said Archie, "one bruise on the back of the head with a lump of wood to you and one black eye with a hefty frying pan to me!"

"I don't know what to say," said John, "I can't thank you enough Sir."

"We'll see about thanks later on," said Billy, "in the meantime Brooklands here we come."

They cut across country through Redhill and Reigate, then right at Dorking, through Leatherhead and finally head to Weybridge and to Brooklands.

They proceeded at a much more leisurely pace than was normal for James, who said, “Nearly there now, just turn right here at Brooklands Road, up the hill and turn left into the Campbell Gate, blimey this takes me back, I had some good fun here before the war.”

They stopped at the gate and Billy spoke to the gatekeeper who directed them to park in what used to be the paddock in front of the old BARC Clubhouse.

“I take it you’ve come here to have a look around Whintons,” said James.

“Exactly James,” said Billy, “although I can’t see that we’re going to find anything untoward there, the manager is extremely trustworthy, as is the staff, so the only weak link is old Whinton who Uncle Bob purchased the business from in the 30’s, unless he has any surviving relatives with a grudge which I would have thought unlikely as he wasn’t married, he was just a sad old chap getting on a bit who didn’t have the energy to keep the place going properly.”

“It’s a shame to see Brooklands quite so run down,” said James, “it was so full of life in the 30’s.”

“And death, I seem to remember,” said Billy.

“Yes, there were quite a few who went over the top into the trees, but you tend not to think of that when you’re young, it’s the same with war, it’s always going to be the other chap who cops it, not you, anyway I’m going to take you all on a guided tour," said James.

"As you know all motor racing stopped at the outbreak of war and sadly never started up again here afterwards, this place was the first purpose built racing circuit in Britain and we're in front of what used to be the Clubhouse for the BARC, the Brooklands Automobile Racing Club, now here's the history lesson, it was built 1907 by Hugh Locke King."

"That's enough history for now," said James, "let's look at the exciting bit," and with that he turned to his right and started walking towards the track which was a couple of hundred yards away.

When they reached the bottom of the track, they could see it disappearing away to their right under a bridge and swooping off into the distance to their left, it was very bumpy and became steeper the further it got to the top.

"Blow me down," said Archie, "it's much steeper than it looks when you get close up, it's hard to believe you raced here in your Bentley."

"This part is called the Members Banking, try and walk up it to the top Archie."

They all had a go and started sliding down as they got towards the top, then James said, "try going backwards you've more chance of getting to the top," which helped no end and they all reached the top of the banking.

"It's like walking up a wall," said Chris, "Lord only knows what it must have been like if you went over the top?"

"I'm glad to say I never found out, I don't think anyone went over and lived, it must have been a brief moment of terror followed by nothing as you slammed into a tree, the thing is you could go faster at the top, that's why the little Austin Ulsters and slower cars were at the bottom and the Bentleys and the like would thunder round at the top," said James, "happy days!"

As they walked back down towards the Clubhouse, James said, "that's enough reminiscing from me," but as they got closer the Clubhouse they were passing a series of wooden buildings on their right, "that shed over there used to be the office and workshop of the famous record breaker Malcolm Campbell, he's not there now of course."

"Did he die then," said John, "I know so many of them did."

"No," said James, "I'm fairly certain he's still alive although he must be getting on a bit now, he must be over sixty I would think, you're right though there's not many record breakers get to that age."

By this time after the war Brooklands had been taken over by Vickers the aircraft manufactures and the Clubhouse had been taken over as offices and design rooms and Billy went in through the double doors at the front and said to the girl on reception, "Mr Trubshaw to see Mr Wallis."

"Very good Sir," said the receptionist, "he is expecting you; would you care to make your own way up?"

"Certainly," said Billy as he led the way through the back of reception, down the corridor and up the flight of stairs to the office of Barnes Wallis where he knocked and entered.

It was a very large and sumptuous office and Barnes stood up to greet them and said, "hello Billy, I was expecting to see Bob when I got the message a Mr Trubshaw was coming to see me, I see you have brought some friends, do all pull up some chairs and make yourselves at home and what can I do for you?"

"Thank you," said Billy, "well it's quite a long story, by the way chaps this is Barnes Wallis for the benefit of those of you who didn't recognise him."

"Good Lord," said John, "Dam Busters, bouncing bomb, that Barnes Wallis!"

"Yes indeed," said Barnes modestly.

"That wasn't his only invention either," said Billy, "it was Barnes that invented the criss-cross trellis structure on the Wellington bomber, what was it called?"

"Geodetic," said Barnes, "it was called Geodetic, the

criss-cross design meant that any plane with this design could take an enormous amount of damage and still retain its structural rigidity, I'd like to think that one or two airmen owe their lives to the design."

"It's funny that people tend to think of Brooklands as a motor racing circuit," said James, "but there was a massive aircraft manufacturing factory here during the war."

"That's right," said Barnes who by now had overcome his modesty as they were discussing some of his favourite subjects, "the Wellington was built here by Vickers-Armstrong, there were thousands of people working here during the war, I myself was here working for Vickers, when I designed the Wellington, in fact they let me use their sea trials tank for my experiments with the bouncing bomb we used on the Dam Busters Raid."

"You see," he continued, "the bouncing bomb was like a pebble that you might skim across a pond, you see the pebble had to be spinning for it to work and that's where I got to know Bob Trubshaw for together we designed the mechanism for spinning the bomb before its release."

"Yes," said Billy and it was Whintons who made the bearings for it to spin on and the release mechanism, I know Uncle Bob was extremely proud of that particular piece of design."

"You know," said Barnes now fully warmed up on the

subject, "we used to test down at Chesil Beach in Dorset, the first bombs were cased in wood but they kept disintegrating when they hit the water, then we made some like enormous metal golf balls to no avail either, then finally we just made the bomb like a giant oil drum, for you see it wasn't the shape but the fact it was spinning sufficiently fast that made it bounce across the water, it had to be spinning backwards you see!"

"Didn't they form a special Squadron to drop the thing," said Archie.

"Yes they did," said Barnes, "617 Squadron, they were based at Scampton in Lincolnshire, quite an amazing bunch of men, they had to fly at night and at one hundred feet to be under the Radar and then even lower when they dropped the bombs against the Dams, well they were mines really that's how it worked."

"The principal was quite simple really," he continued, "you skim the bomb across the lake to get close to the Dam where it slides down under water and then explodes, the force of the explosion is magnified by the mass of water which pushes the explosion against the Dam wall, that's the easy bit, the clever part is getting the planes there in the pitch dark without crashing or being shot down, then flying low enough to drop the bomb in exactly the right place to skim the bomb over the surface and then escape and get home alive, 617 Squadron did the clever part."

“Amazingly enough they managed to destroy the Mohne and the Eder and damage the Sorpe sufficient to stop all German industrial production in the Ruhr Valley for months, they said it shortened the war considerably,” said Barnes, “my only regret was the loss of life, unfortunately we lost 53 of the 133 of our chaps that took part, I wasn’t expecting that.”

“They must have been very brave men,” said Christopher.

“Yes they were, after the raid 617 Squadron took the motto, Apres Moi Le Deluge,” said Barnes, “After me the deluge, very apt don’t you think, ironically on the night of the raid, Squadron Leader Guy Gibson’s dog Nigger was run over and killed just outside the airfield gate and Gibson himself was killed later in a plane crash but I suppose that’s war for you.”

“The best thing about the raid though was the Air Ministry becoming positive about my Earthquake bombs which I was having trouble getting the green light for, the RAF sunk the Turpitz with a couple of my 6-ton Tallboy bombs,” said Barnes.

“Oh yes,” said James,” Archie and I are very familiar with the Turpitz, good for you Sir”

“I’m currently working on a brand new project,” said Barnes, “just round the corner I have a Stratosphere Chamber in which we can simulate the conditions experienced when flying at high altitude,” he paused and said, "I'm awfully sorry chaps, here I am waffling on about all this and I expect you actually came with some purpose in mind, do forgive me."

"That's perfectly fine Sir, I'm sure we all found your stories extremely interesting, I certainly did," said Billy, "and I did have a purpose in coming to see you but you've answered one of my questions already."

"What might that be then Billy?" said Barnes.

"Well, Uncle Bob has disappeared but I can tell from the fact that you were expecting to see him and not me that you have no idea of his whereabouts."

"I certainly don't," said Barnes, "I had thought it a little odd that he hadn't popped in to see me when he visited Whintons but I'm usually so engrossed in my work I would have no idea when I last saw him but it's very nice to see you Billy and your friends."

"Yes," said Billy, "I'm sorry to barge in with quite so many people, let me introduce them, this is James Arbuthnott, his father is a good friend of Uncle Bob and this is his associate Archibald Cluff and they are private detectives who are trying to help me find Uncle Bob."

"The other chaps are John Spearman and Christopher Brown," said Billy, "I can get down to their story later."

"Well, it's very nice to meet you all," said Barnes, "any friend of Billy's is a friend of mine, I don't suppose you'd care to join me for lunch, we have a perfectly respectable canteen here, I'd be delighted if you would all join me."

They all followed Barnes towards the canteen and Billy said, "go on ahead chaps, I'm just going to pop in and see our Manager at Whintons, I'll catch you up, I won't be long, I'll have whatever's going and a cup of tea."

Barnes led them into a rather massive canteen and said, "we operate the canteen rather like the British Restaurants during the war, fairly decent food at moderate prices, we don't want our chaps collapsing over their lathes from malnutrition."

As they all sat down a waitress dressed in black, rather in the style of a Lyons Corner House Nippy came to serve them, she was wearing a black frock with a white collar and a white apron with a black and white headband to keep her hair tidy and looked very smart.

"Good morning Mr Wallis," she said, "and what can I get for you today?"

"Well, it looks like six for lunch," said Barnes "and six teas, please."

The waitress scurried away and was soon back with six dishes of soup, "leak and potato today Sir," she said as she placed the soup on the table.

"Just in time," said Billy as he joined them at the table.

"Any luck at the factory?" asked James.

"I'm afraid not, I've drawn a complete blank there, I spoke to the manager, he has no idea where Uncle Bob may be, nor why he might have disappeared, he's checked all the records, there's no-one at the factory who's been fired or has a grudge, so I think we can rule out any connection with the factory."

The second course of chicken and two veg arrived and although the portions were not large, they were adequate, "this is splendid," said Chris, "I'm amazed how large this canteen is, there must be thousands of people working here."

"There certainly were during the war but not quite so many now, that's why I sneak in early for lunch as it tends to get a little noisy in here when it's busy," said Barnes, "I suggest we hurry with the cheese and biscuits before the rush, we can go back to the office and finish our chat." He paid the bill and left sixpence tip and called out to the waitress, "Goodbye Gladys, thank you."

Back in the office as they sat down again and Billy said, "thanks awfully for lunch Barnes we all enjoyed it tremendously and now I'm afraid I'm going to prevail upon your generosity once again if I may."

"Certainly, how can I help?" said Barnes.

"Without putting too fine a point on it, these two chaps

here are in need of an honest job," said Billy as he gestured towards John and Chris. "They're both just demobbed and both drivers and I'm willing to recommend them to you, I'm sure they will turn out to be model employees."

Barnes took some paper from his desk and started writing with his fountain pen, "Well if you are willing to recommend them, that's good enough for me, I'm sure we can find them something to start with in the stores and who knows what from there, especially as they can both drive."

He put the note into an envelope and said, "take this letter and go and see the foreman of the stores, my secretary will show you the way, he'll sort out jobs for you both and can probably arrange some digs for you as well and good luck to you chaps."

"I can't tell you how grateful we are Sir, we won't let you down," said John, "and to you too Mr Trubshaw."

As they left the office to find the foreman, James called to them, "good luck both of you and may I suggest next time you fancy a boat trip you stick to the boating lake."

"We will Sir," said Chris as they left the room.

"Thank you for that Barnes," said Billy, "it's been wonderful seeing you again but we'd better be making our way home now."

"My pleasure," said Barnes, "I'm sure you can find your way out, do let me know as soon as you have news of Bob won't you."

"Of course, we will," said Billy as they all said their goodbye's and went back down to the car to head for home.

That night after dinner they all gathered in the drawing room for drinks, Billy rang the bell which was near the fireplace hanging on the wall and said, "I think it safe to say we had a fairly constructive day and we have found work for our two young chaps who I think will make a decent fist of the rest of their lives, perhaps that's an excuse for Champagne."

"Yes," said Jane, "I had a lovely day today too, it's the first time I've been able to relax since Bob went missing, I think some Champagne would do us all good.

A moment later a portion of the bookcase which was opposite to the fireplace opened to reveal Wilson the Butler carrying a heavy silver try under his arm, he took their order for Champagne and disappeared back through the bookcase door.

"That's clever," said Archie, "I hadn't even realised there was a hidden door there."

"Yes, there are a few of them about the house," said Jane, "they are there so the staff can move about the house without being seen, should there be important guests in the house, you wouldn't want the Duke of Windsor catching a maid cleaning, would you."

"Quite right," said Billy, "how was your day Amelia, I hope it was as useful as ours, did you get the telegram you were expecting?"

"We had a lovely day, thank you," said Amelia, "and I did received the telegram I was hoping for but it wasn't quite the news I was expecting so Jane and I went for a drive in her delightful little car, we had a smashing day and a cream tea for good measure."

"But no good news with the telegram," said James.

"Not what I was hoping for," she said, "I was researching the family tree of Lord Eddleton as you asked and it took much longer than I expected and is a rather sad story as it turned out, but I'd better start at the beginning."

Your Grandfather Herbert Trubshaw became a very successful businessman and purchased Brightmoor from Lord Eddleton in 1868 not long after he had started Hamwells, the Department store in Knightsbridge.

"Yes, that's right," said Billy, "unfortunately the son of Lord Eddleton drunk excessively and had racked up enormous gambling debts but his father was an honourable man and sold Brightmoor to pay off his son's debts, unfortunately the shame of it was too much for him and Lord Eddleton who was getting on a bit died not long afterwards.

"I believe your Grandfather gave the surviving wife a cottage on the estate," said Amelia, "and she lived there until her death."

The bookcase door opened again and Wilson stepped into the room with the Champagne and glasses on the tray.

"Oh, you made me jump," said Amelia.

"Do forgive me Madam," said Wilson as he served the Champagne and left the room.

"Now, where was I," said Amelia, "ah yes, Lord Eddleton's son was a little harder to trace," said Amelia, "I had to rely heavily on Parish records and it seems he had a son called Donald with a local girl in 1876 but I could find no record of a wedding certificate."

"Donald, however went on to have a son called Henry in 1898 and I found death certificates for both his parents, the father died fairly young at the age of thirty two shortly after Donald's birth, said Amelia, "it was quite a paper chase but with Jane's help we got there."

"I also found records for Henry who entered the Army in 1914 aged sixteen and also a record of his death in August 1916 in the Battle of the Somme," said Amelia, "there were no records of a wife or any surviving relatives."

"Well done and thank you, Amelia and Jane, you've both done some sterling work there," said James, "most useful and one which leads me on to my next course of action which will require a visit to Calais."

"Why Calais," said Billy, "I don't see the connection."

"There isn't one," replied James, "but we seem to have eliminated any likely suspects who might have wanted to harm Uncle Billy from his past, no-one has a grudge from either the purchase of Brightmoor nor the acquisition of Whintons so we have to look elsewhere and the only loose end seems to have something to do with Blackbird and Calais, so tomorrow I suggest a trip to Calais.

A JOLLY UP TO CALAIS.

James, had been in the dining room having breakfast with Jane, Amelia and Archie when he was called to the phone in the entrance hall by the stairs, he was talking as Billy passed on his way to breakfast.

"Hello George, you obviously got the message," said James as he paused, "that's right George, thank you for that' I'll leave it in your capable hands, if I need you I will call you, don't call me back until after the weekend we're having a little trip to Calais," he paused again, "thank you, and you enjoy your weekend too, goodbye."

As he finished his phone call, he joined Billy who was coming down the stairs and they went in to join the others in the dining room and having served themselves they sat at the table and ate breakfast.

When he'd finished breakfast James said, "Archie and I have a little errand to run before we can leave for Calais, I'm sure we can leave everything in your capable hands Billy, we have left some cases with Wilson if you can make sure they get to the boat we will meet you all in Folkstone."

"Excellent," said Billy, "leave it to me see you in Folkstone."

As they drove away from Brightmoor, Archie turned to James and said, "I suppose it would be a silly question to ask where we're going?"

"Not at all silly Archie," said James, "we're going to Maidstone and thanks to George and his access to phone books I can even tell you the road we are looking for, it's Vileas Way and it should be easy enough to spot as we go into Maidstone it's on the right so I'm led to believe."

"And the reason for our visit to Maidstone," said Archie.

"Well we're on the way to Folkstone harbour to pick up the Blackbird to go to Calais," said James, "so obviously we need to pick up a Captain."

"Of course," said Archie, who was none the wiser but got the map out and said, "it's a pretty straight route from here, I'll shout when we're looking for Vilias Way," and with that James put his foot down and the Bentley roared into life.

As usual with James, it wasn't long before they were entering the outskirts of Maidstone and Archie called out, "there, there on the right Vilias Way."

As they turned into the road James said, "we're looking for St Vilias Rest Home, you look your side and I'll look mine."

They were soon parking on the semi-circular drive outside St Vileas Rest Home which was a very imposing looking brick-built building, with a large white painted porch under which they stopped the car, switched off the engine and entered the reception.

"I still don't understand," said Archie.

"You soon will," said James as he asked the receptionist if it would be possible to visit a Mrs Ruth Babbows, if you could tell her it's James Atbuthnott to see her."

"I'm not sure Sir," said the receptionist, "she's a bit reclusive, in fact I don't think she's come out of her room since she booked in, I'll call her and see if she's taking visitors, it won't take a moment."

Putting the phone down the receptionist said, "well it seems you're in luck Sir, her room is just down the corridor there it's number 11, she said to go straight in."

James led Archie down the corridor to room 11, knocked on the door and entered to see a gentleman standing in front of the bay window looking out, "hello

Bob," he said.

The man turned and said, "hello James, I thought you would have found me sooner but I'm still very glad to see you none the less, I tried to leave you the clues with young Billy, obviously he contacted you."

"Yes he did and with the note saying you were in St Ives," said James, "and it reminded me of just how bad you were at doing crosswords, I have to say they were some of the worst anagrams I've seen for a long time, however they did the job, when I knew you were here, I didn't have to hurry as I knew you were safe, I mean who on earth would come looking for a Ruth Babbows in St Vilias Rest Home."

"It's just as well someone did," said Archie.

"Have you come to take me home," said Bob, "is it safe."

"I think you're safe enough now you're with us," said James, "and anyway we need a Captain for Blackbird, we're on our way to Calais and don't ask," he paused, "I'll explain on the way, we don't want to miss the tide."

Bob quickly packed his bag and was ready to leave when James said, "come on Ruth, time to pay the bill and leave."

"Sorry about that," said Bob, "I couldn't for the life of me work out another name."

"If I were you," said James, "I'd stick to engineering, quite clearly you're never going to make a code breaker, oh by the way we met Barnes yesterday, he sent his regards."

"Oh, that's marvellous, I must pop in and see him when I next get the chance," said Bob.

Jumping in the Bentley they set off for Folkstone Harbour, James said, "it will be good for Jane to see you and for all of us to have a relaxing weekend away."

"I'm so sorry I didn't manage to let her know I was alright," said Bob, "but I didn't have the time before I went into hiding and afterwards, I thought it best not to draw attention to myself."

"Someone sent me the ridiculous threatening letter," continued Bob, "GIVE ME MY SHARE, OR YOU WILL DIE, cut out of pieces from the newspaper, like a cheap crime novel and then farmer Smith was killed wearing my hat, I thought these people are serious so I disappeared, it was obviously me they were after and I didn't want Jane in danger."

"As you say, someone is after you but as yet we don't know who or why, I have a funny feeling the murder of farmer Smith was a case of mistaken identity, although we've eliminated the two chaps who tried to steal Blackbird," said James, "all we can do now is follow the trail to wherever it leads and the next step must be Calais."

When they arrived at the Harbour and pulled up by the Blackbird, Jane was standing on the aft deck and on seeing that Bob was in the car with James and Archie she rushed down the gangplank and ran into Bob's waiting arms.

"Bob," she cried out, "I thought you were dead, I really thought you were dead and then I kept seeing you at home, I didn't know what was going on," she kissed him and said, "I love you Bob."

"I know you do, old girl," said Bob, "I love you too, now let's get aboard and have a lovely weekend in Calais just like we used to."

The crew was made up of a Captain and five others but Bob used to pilot the boat whenever he could and as he started the engines of Blackbird the crew cast off and they were on their way to Calais with Bob at the helm, "I'll just radio the Harbourmaster and let him know where we're going and to expect us back on Monday," he said as he steered out through the Harbour entrance and out into the open sea.

"Just a quick word everyone," said Bob, " do try to keep an eye out for mines, they have cleared the majority of them and we are following the route of the Boat Train so we should be fine but just in case we spot a loose one, just call out , Mine!" "Now everyone, go and make yourselves at home and enjoy the facilities aboard Blackbird."

"Would you mind if I stayed here with you in the wheelhouse," asked Archie.

"Certainly," said Bob, "be my guest, Billy would you be good enough to take the others below to the salon, it will be much more comfortable for them down there."

It was a beautiful day and they had been at sea for about an hour and a half, it was almost flat calm and Bob even allowed Archie to take the wheel for a little while which he enjoyed immensely, when Archie suddenly shouted "Mine!"

Bob turned the Blackbird hard-a-port and narrowly missed the mine, "this one must have come loose from its mooring and is just floating with the tide, I'd better warn the coastguard to alert other shipping."

Jane on hearing all the commotion appeared on deck and realising what was going on went back below only to appear again with her hunting rifle, complete with sights and grabbed a heavy mahogany chair from the deck towards the railing on the starboard side and resting the rifle on the top rail started to adjust the sights.

Bob called down from the wheelhouse, "I'll try and hold station here, we don't want to be too close when that thing goes up, it's a hell of a shot Jane dear but you've got to hit the spikes which are sticking out of the mine."

Jane took aim and shot three times, each time adjusting

the sights, "lucky it's flat calm today," she said, "I'm sure I can do this," and after another two shots she was right, there was the most almighty explosion which shot a plume of water high into the air.

"Well done, old girl," shouted Bob, "lucky you brought your gun, better keep it out of sight when we get to Calais though, I'm not sure if it would impress the French Police."

"I will," said Jane, "with things as they are at the moment it seemed like a good idea to bring it with us on this trip."

A couple of hours later as it approached late afternoon, they were entering Calais Harbour and tied up at the quayside and James exclaimed, "it's so sad to see Calais has been so badly damaged, it looks like so many towns all over England and Europe, all trying to pick themselves up and start again."

"Yes indeed," said Bob, "I wasn't expecting them to get up and running so quickly but I'm delighted that they have, this takes me back to the wonderful trips we used to have before the war."

"I hadn't expected this it's such a shame, the Old Town here was so pretty, I remember when I came with you to Le Mans when I was a lad and they used to hoist the cars off the deck of the ships to the quayside," said James, "so what's next on the itinerary?"

"We usually have afternoon tea here on the boat," said Bob, "and later we head into town and eat at the Hotel de Paris which is on the Rue De Madrid, the seafood there is superb and the Maître D has the most wonderful collection of wines, which amazingly enough they managed to hide from the Nazis for the entire duration of the war, I'm really looking forward to our return again and then tomorrow we shall fly down to Le Touquet for a spot of fun."

The aft deck was covered by an awning with open sides and had been laid for afternoon tea which was served by the two crewmen, "how frightfully British we must look," said Amelia.

"Very true," said Billy, "but I see nothing wrong with that."

"Agreed," said Amelia, "you can't beat a good cuppa!"

When tea was finished Bob said, "I suggest a quick wash and brush up and we can head off to the Hotel for dinner," and with that they all got up to ready themselves for the evening meal.

Archie and James were the first ready followed by Bob and Billy and then finally Amelia and Jane who as usual looked quite stunning in a dark blue cocktail dress with a black fox fur wrap, they all followed Bob down the gangplank and off into Calais town to the Hotel.

Just like London there were many bomb sites and

damaged buildings where homes and businesses had once been but considering they had been occupied by the Germans during the war who had ransacked the place it was good to see any progress in getting back to normal.

Upon arrival they entered the lobby and went straight to the restaurant where they were met by the Maître D, Jean Leroux who said, "bon soir, bon soir, good evening Monsieur Bob and the delightful Jane and Monsieur Billy, how pleased I am to see you again."

"Thank you, Jean," said Bob as he introduced Alfie, James and Amelia, "I have to say it's a delight to be here too."

"Do please follow me, I have some Champagne already waiting for you," said Jean as he led them to a table and opened two bottles of Champagne and served them, "I'm afraid the menu is a little limited from what you may remember before the war but the fish is still to be recommended, it is all freshly caught today."

"Thank you," said Bob, "I'm sure we will all find something to suit us, although as Archie is a little fussy with his food I shall not be recommending the fish soup for him especially as I seem to remember you leave the heads on."

"Might I suggest perhaps Croquette de Poisson," said Jean.

"What might that be?" said Archie.

"Fish cakes!" said James.

"That 'ill do for me," said Archie.

"So, we have it now Jean," said Bob, "one for fish cakes, two for the lobster, two for crab and one for the sole, thank you."

Billy checked all the Champagne glasses were full and stood up to propose a toast, "ladies and gentlemen I give you Mr Bob Trubshaw and his safe return to normal life."

They all stood and raised a glass to Bob, who said, "thank you, I must say I'm delighted to be back too."

Jean returned a little later carrying two bottles of wine, "your usual wine Sir," he said.

"Thank you, Jean, that will be excellent," said Bob, "I know it's traditional to have white with fish and red with meat but this red is so good we drink it with everything it really is superb."

Having polished off their dinner and another couple of bottles of wine it was time to depart for the Blackbird for the night, so Bob paid the bill and they all said goodbye to Jean.

"Before you go Monsieur Bob," said Jean, "I took the liberty of sending three crates of your favourite wine down to the boat, that's two for you and one for my brother Henri at the Imperial if you would be so kind as to deliver it for me as usual."

"Certainly," said Bob, "it will be my pleasure."

When they arrived back at the boat, a crewman met them as they came up the gangplank, "the Hotel de Paris has delivered three cases of wine for you Sir, we have stored it down below for safe keeping, will there be anything else tonight?"

"I think the ladies are going to turn in but if you could arrange a bottle of Port in the Salon for myself and the chaps, that will be all," said Bob, "thank you."

The crewman said goodnight and disappeared below to deliver the Port to the Salon.

Bob poured them all large glasses of Port and as they sat down Archie said, "this really is a beautiful boat, my father was a carpenter, not up to this standard but I can really appreciate the inlaid wooden panels and the superb standard of workmanship."

"Yes, it is a magnificent boat and not long back from recommissioning by Goole's, I'm very lucky to have her," said Bob, "but it's really my father Herbert who started all this that both Billy and myself have to thank for our good fortune," he raised his glass and said, "gentlemen, I ask you to be upstanding as I give you Herbert Trubshaw."

When they sat down Billy asked, "do you wish to see anything special tomorrow James?"

"Yes, I do," said James, "exactly as today, I want to see everything you normally do when you're over for a weekend trip, I'm sure that the clues as to what's happening with Bob are somehow there, we just haven't seen then yet"

"In that case," said Bob, "we shall have an early breakfast, here on the boat, then we have a car to take us to the airport for the fairly short flight down to Le Touquet, we should arrive in time for luncheon, we're staying at Le Westminster and then perhaps a little trip to the Casino in the evening."

"That sound interesting," said Archie, "I've never been in a Casino before."

"I'm certain you will enjoy it," said Bob, "but make sure you don't lose your shirt, I've seen more than one man ruin his life by gambling."

"I shall be very careful Sir," said Archie, "I never used to play cards before I joined the Army but then it became a way of taking your mind off things before going into action, we played an awful lot of cards on the way over for the St Nazaire raid, I remember but it was only for pennies, sadly there weren't too many chaps who got to keep their winnings on that raid."

"Yes, Billy did mention that you both were on that raid,"

said Bob, filling all their glasses and raising his as a toast, "to all the brave men and women who didn't manage to get back."

They finished their drinks and Billy said "goodnight all," and went to bed leaving Bob, Archie And James to follow behind, "Goodnight chaps," said Bob, "and don't forget Archie, we'll be dressing for dinner tomorrow night."

"Yes, I have been warned," said Archie, as he and James followed on to their bedrooms.

The following morning continental breakfast was served under the awning on the aft deck and consisted of a selection of cold meat, cheese, croissants, fruit, coffee and freshly made French bread from the local boulangerie, "this is different," said Archie.

"When in Rome," replied Billy, "do as the Romans do!"

It was a beautiful morning and Amelia and Jane were both resplendent in Summer frocks and James and Archie were wearing Linen suits, one dark and one light, whereas Bob and Billy had tailored Mohair suits of differing hues, "my, don't we all look smart today," said Jane, "I think we should cut the mustard in Le Touquet, don't you think Billy?"

"I certainly do," said Billy.

A very large but rather old Delage shooting brake

together with driver was parked on the quayside with the engine running, the two crewmen took the suitcases and placed them on the rack on top of the car, whilst the entire party followed down the gangplank towards the waiting car.

"I'm surprised to see there are still cars about, you wouldn't have thought so many would have survived," said Archie.

"When you think about it," said James, "there's two reasons for that, rather like the wine last night which was hidden, they also hid the cars if they could and the ones that were left were commandeered by the Germans for their own use so that would account for a lot of the survivors, although I would imagine an awful lot of the best things were packed up and sent back to Germany, never to be seen again."

The seating arrangement in the Delage was such that Bob sat in the back with Jane and Amelia on either side and James, Archie and Billy were on the fold down seats in front of them.

Billy tapped on the separating glass and gestured to the driver they were ready to leave and as the car drew away he glanced behind to see Bob between Jane and Amelia and said, "I would normally use the old expression, a rose between two thorns but in this case it is most certainly, a thorn between two delightful roses."

“How kind,” said Jane, “you three chaps have scrubbed up quite well too.”

The airport was only a matter of a few miles outside town so it wasn’t long before they were stopping outside the small terminal which was an Art Deco building painted white and was gleaming in the morning sun shine and while a porter took their cases to the plane they all entered the terminal where Bob went to deal with the paperwork whilst the others sat in the waiting area.

When he had finished Bob came over and said, “they’re ready for us now, we can board the plane whenever we’re ready,” and he led the way out of the terminal and out to where the plane was waiting on the grass runway.

The plane was a rather splendid twin engine De Haviland Dragon Rapide bi plane with eight seats which had a set of steps to the rear of the port wing which they used to step onto the wing and then into the cabin, “this is rather good fun,” said Archie, as he stepped onto the wing and the captain said, “watch your head when entering the cabin Sir.”

When they were all aboard and seated the Captain started the engines and radioed the tower for clearance for take-off, he revved the engines slightly and taxied slowly to the end of the runway where he opened up the engines and the plane increased speed bumping along the grass until eventually they could feel it leave the ground.

The sun was on their port side as they flew South West towards Le Touquet, the windows on the plane were large and gave a splendid view of the sea below which was a bright blue and was glistening in the sunshine, "doesn't the sea look wonderful, makes you want to have a dip," said Amelia, to which Bob replied, "yes, but I can tell you from experience, it's colder than it looks, it's such a shame to see the bomb craters and the damage from up here, especially as I can remember what it was like when we used to fly down pre-war."

"We used to fly over from England with our friend Ronald Waters and his wife, he had a plane like this and used to keep it at Gatwick," said Bob, "he formed the Surrey Aero Club there, it was close to the Gatwick Horseracing Course, so we could meet and lose a few bob on the horses and then try and win it back in the Casino in Le Touquet," he paused, "I must say we very rarely did, but it was always a rather good jolly up!"

It was a fairly short hop down the coast to Le Touquet so it wasn't long before they were landing and retrieving their cases for the drive to the rather splendid Le Westminster Hotel, another Art Deco building which was built in 1924, "I'm so delighted to see the old place still standing," said Bob, as the car drew to a halt outside the hotel, "too many of them have succumbed to the ravages of war and I'm particularly partial to this one, it holds a lot of good memories of days gone by."

When they entered the lobby, the manager rushed over to welcome Bob and Jane, saying how delighted he was to see them again, he gathered everyone together and directed them to the cocktail bar for complimentary Champagne while he went to get the keys for their rooms.

As they sat and the waiter brought the Champagne Archie said, "this is the sort of life I could get used to," and Billy replied, "not at these prices, you couldn't!"

"You've got a point Billy," said Archie, "I feel a bit of a fraud being here at your Uncle's expense when we don't appear to be doing very much to solve the riddle of who is threatening him, I feel a little like an overpaid baby sitter."

"Believe me Archie," replied Bob, "I'm only too happy to have you and James here as overpaid baby sitters, both Jane and I feel a great deal safer knowing you are both here looking after me."

They ordered another bottle of Champagne and having drunk it headed in for luncheon and having had the menu translated by Amelia, Archie plumped for a mushroom omelette which was specially prepared for him and after lunch they made their way to their rooms which were next to each other on the first floor.

"I'm having a bit of a nap and a long bath before

dinner," said Bob, "this should give you plenty of time to get ready Archie, don't forget this is Le Touquet, and we shall be dressing for dinner."

James and Archie were sharing a twin room and next to them were Bob and Jane, with Amelia next and lastly Billy and as they entered their rooms Archie said, "I think it was wise to have Amelia on the other side, I have a feeling she could handle herself should a situation occur."

"Well I suggest we have a bath fairly soon," said James, "as I have a feeling it's going to take you some time fiddling with the shirt studs to get the job done in time," and after a bath and a fair amount of swearing Archie was finally ready to go on parade.

They both looked very smart as they went down to the bar before dinner, "thanks for doing the tie," said Archie, "lord only knows how you tie one of those things, I couldn't find the last loop for love nor money, I don't know how you do it."

"Like most things in life," said James, "it's just a matter of practice, you weren't the best shot in the Battalion when you first started, were you?"

They entered the lift and the operator shut the outer door and then the inner which was a sliding metal grid and Archie commented, "blimey, that's just like the Geodetic thing Barnes Wallis designed, I wonder if that's where he got the idea from?"

"I have no idea," said James, "but I do know he put it to damn good use in the Wellington Bomber."

They smiled as the lift doors opened and headed towards the bar to find Billy had beaten them to it, "come and join me," he said, "I've ordered Champagne for us all, the others won't be long."

As James and Archie sat the waiter poured them Champagne, "you're getting the hang of this dressing up business," said Billy to Archie, "I think it safe to say you look a proper gentleman."

"Thank you for that," replied Archie, "I don't want to be seen to be letting the side down."

"You're certainly not Archie," said Billy as they all stood as the others came over to join them, all the men looked rather splendid in their dinner jackets and Amelia and Jane both looked stunning as usual in full length evening gowns, one in pink and the other in cream.

They went in for dinner and everyone except for James and Archie drunk more Champagne, "do have some more," said Bob, but Archie replied, "I think it best if we drink in moderation, we are effectively on duty so to speak."

When they were seated at the table, Bob said, "We're so lucky to be here, this is such a wonderful place," and Jane continued, "yes, it was the Duke of Windsor who first put us on to this place, we used to have so much fun here before the war, anyone who was anyone was here, Noel Coward, P.G Wodehouse, do you remember."

"Yes I do," said Bob, "he wrote those marvellous Jeeves and Wooster books, his wife Ethel used to call him Plummie and he used to have a villa here but the silly so and so left it too late to get away before the Germans took the place over."

"Obviously they arrested him and put him in a camp, then they took him to Berlin where he was put in a hotel where he made five broadcasts for the Germans about life in a prison camp, something I think he lived to regret later, then he turned up later in 44 in Paris and when the war was over he went off to America, damn funny books though!"

Dinner was up to the standard one would expect from a hotel of this calibre and Archie had a steak although the others thought it prudent not to mention that it was in fact a steak from a horse, "that was a lovely bit of meat," he said when finished and Jane replied, "I'm very glad you enjoyed it and now I think it's time for the Casino"

It was a balmy summer evening as they walked round the corner to the Casino where Bob and Billy changed a large wad of cash into chips and gave some to Jane and Amelia and were about to give some to Archie when

James said, " I think we'll just spectate, if you don't mind, we can keep an eye on you better that way, but you enjoy yourselves please."

The Casino was a glorious over decorated building with glass chandeliers which glistened in the many gilt mirrors on the walls, Jane headed for the Roulette wheel, while Bob and Billy went straight to the Poker table leaving Amelia to try her hand at Blackjack, which left James and Archie free to spectate at the Poker table.

Some hours passed and they all met again to cash in their chips, or lack of them in the case of Bob and Billy, however Jane had a handful left which Billy thought was pretty good going until Amelia arrived carrying a silver tray laden with chips, "good Lord," he said, "we never come out of here with anything left, how on earth did you manage that."

Amelia cashed her chips and was looking very pleased with herself, "when I was a singer we used to have plenty of time to spare between shows, or when we were travelling with the bands so the girls and I used to play Pontoon, although I see they call it Blackjack here, but the principal is the same, I don't usually gamble, it must be beginners luck."

When they all left the Casino and were walking back to the Hotel, James caught up with Amelia and walked along with her, "I seem to remember when we first interviewed you for the job you mentioned something about having a bit of a photographic memory, have you ever heard of card counting?"

"Card counting," said Amelia, "card counting, you say," she paused and said, "I couldn't possibly say."

By the time they were back at the hotel it was the early hours of the morning and as they left the lift to go to their rooms Archie said, "I must say it has been an enjoyable night but I won't half be glad to get this collar undone," to which Amelia replied, "if you think that's uncomfortable Archie, you should try being a woman and having to deal with corsets, suspender belts and high heels, then you'd know what uncomfortable is!"

They all laughed and said goodnight and went to their rooms for the night and the following morning after a late breakfast and a little promenade round Le Touquet they all boarded the car for the return trip to the Airport and the flight back to Calais.

During the afternoon, James and Archie took Amelia for a drink in one of the café's frequented by the locals in Calais in the hope of gleaning any information which may help their investigation and although Amelia's fluent French together with her delightful looks led to many a Frenchman wanting to chat, no useful information was forthcoming.

On the way back to the boat Amelia said, "I'm awfully sorry we didn't learn anything but we did our best."

"We certainly did Amelia," said James, "I wouldn't say we didn't learn anything, we learnt that Frenchmen love to be in the company of an attractive and vivacious young woman and Archie has learnt that la plume de ma tante est sur le bureau de mon oncle!"

"I think I will leave the French to you Amelia," said Archie, "especially if I'm looking for the whereabouts of my Aunt's pen."

The evening was spent with a splendid meal prepared on the boat, together with more of the wine brought from the Hotel de Paris and more French lessons from Amelia, including some of the less well-known phrases taught to her by French soldiers during the war.

An early start on Monday and a somewhat less eventful trip back to Folkstone in the Blackbird, much to everyone's relief meant they were home at Brightmoor by mid-morning.

TO CATCH A CROOK.

On arrival back at Brightmoor, Bob said, "That was a wonderful weekend and it's so wonderful to be home and to feel safe, although I'm still in a party mood and I still have to deliver their wine so I suggest luncheon at The Imperial."

Not wishing to disappoint him they all went to get ready and as they went to their rooms James said, "I wonder if I might borrow the telephone," to which Bob replied, "by all means old chap, use the one in the study if you need to be private."

The chaps had a quick wash and brush up and were soon waiting downstairs for the ladies who had done a complete change and were looking radiant as usual, "well, there's a sight," said Bob, "and one well worth waiting for."

Williams arrived outside in the Daimler and Bob

checked the boot of the car to see the wine was safely aboard, once again he was between Jane and Amelia in the back leaving the boys in the folding seats, “The Imperial Hotel, Tunbridge Wells please Williams,” said Bob and they were away.

After a very pleasant drive through the countryside they were entering the outskirts of Tunbridge Wells and as they drove slowly through the town various people who noticed the car would tip their hat in acknowledgement of Bob and Jane.

The Imperial Hotel was an imposing Victorian building in the centre of town and William the Chauffeur halted the car right outside the front entrance and Bob led the way into the lobby of the Hotel where he was greeted by a somewhat perplexed Henri Leroux who was the Manager of the Hotel.

“Good afternoon Sir, how nice to see you,” said Henri, “we weren’t expecting you, I heard you had gone away.”

“Yes, I was away for a while,” said Bob, “but I’m back now and we’d rather like luncheon for six if you don’t mind.”

“Certainly Sir,” said Henri, as he led them into the dining room, seated them and brought menus, “obviously your favourite wine Sir,” he questioned.

“Yes please,” said Bob, “by the way we’ve just been

over to see your brother in Calais, I have another case of wine he asked me to drop in to you, I'll get William to bring it in after luncheon."

The Imperial Hotel was renowned for its roast beef and Yorkshire pudding luncheon and the beef generally came from one of the farms on the Brightmoor estate, "that's one of the perks of living in the countryside," said Bob, "you can always get some decent food if you're willing to pay for it and I would certainly recommend the beef."

Salmon pate was decided on to start by all except Archie who went for the vegetable soup and again when the others settled on the roast beef, Archie a man who couldn't resist a pie, plumped for steak and kidney, they all enjoyed the wine and ordered coffee to finish.

Henri was overseeing the coffee service when Inspector Andrews came into the restaurant together with Sergeant Collins and a Constable who was carrying the case of wine from the boot of the car, "my name is Inspector Andrews, the building is surrounded and I would like you all to remain exactly where you are."

"How dare you Inspector," said Henri, "you can't come in here upsetting my customers like this, I'm going to have to ask you to leave."

"I'm afraid not Sir," said the Inspector, turning to James, "here is the wine from the boot of the car as you asked."

“Do forgive this intrusion,” said James as he addressed the diners in the restaurant, “I’m afraid a crime has been committed and we need to get to the bottom of it,” he paused and then asked one of the waitresses to go to the kitchen and fetch a soup tureen and a fine sieve which she duly did and on returning placed on the dining table.

James turned to Henri and said, “I wonder if you would be so kind as to open one of the bottles of wine, we have just brought back from your brother in Calais.”

“I don’t see the point,” protested Henri, as he opened a bottle.

“Bear with me,” said James as he took the opened bottle and poured it through the sieve into the tureen.

“I really must protest, I see no reason for opening the wine like this,” said Henri, “as you can see there is nothing wrong with the wine.”

“Another bottle please,” said James and he poured the second bottle through the sieve, this time however the sieve was not empty but contained a quantity of rather fine diamonds.

James turned to the Inspector and said, “I would ask you Inspector to arrest this man for diamond smuggling and for theft.”

The Inspector looked quizzically at James who said, “yes

of course Inspector, an explanation," he paused briefly and then continued, "diamond jewellery is stolen all across Europe and is taken to Antwerp where it is dismantled or recut to be transported to Calais where they are placed in the wine bottles which are then innocently brought here by Bob Trubshaw as a favour to his friend Jean Leroux at the Hôtel de Paris, and once here they are made up into new pieces and sold by unscrupulous dealers in Hatton Garden."

"I really must protest," said Henri, "this has nothing to do with me, it must be my brother Jean, I am innocent."

"I'm afraid not Sir," said James, "one of my associates has been recording your telephone conversations and has handed the evidence to the Police in London and your brother is not implicated in any way, I have also taken the liberty of notifying the French and Belgium Police, I imagine Scotland Yard will follow up on Hatton Garden."

"I think this will also explain why our two unfortunate soldiers were caught up in the plot to steal the Blackbird," said James, "as on your last voyage you mistakenly delivered the wrong case of wine to Henri here who went about trying to trace the other case which contained the last shipment of diamonds."

"Right then," said The Inspector, "Henri Leroux, I'm arresting you for theft and diamond smuggling, take him to the station Constable and read him his rights."

"Well done Inspector," said Bob, "it's not every day you catch an international jewel thief, you and Sergeant Collins must come back to Brightmoor with us for a little celebration."

The Inspector, who was feeling rather pleased with himself said, "thank you Sir, that's very kind of you I'm sure."

Constable Lamb handcuffed Henri and led him out to the waiting Black Maria and Sergeant Collins and Inspector Andrews took the Wolsey Police car and followed behind the Trushaw's Daimler back to Brightmoor.

On arrival Billy escorted Jane and Amelia into the Drawing Room and Archie and Bob followed behind whilst James waited for the Inspector and Sergeant Collins, "quite a day Inspector," said James.

"It certainly is Sir," said the Inspector, "I have to say I have never arrested an International jewel thief before, that'll show 'em back at Scotland Yard, thank you for your assistance Sir, I couldn't have done it without you."

"Yes Inspector, I'm sure you're right, now do come inside and have a celebratory drink," said James as he led the two of them into the house and into the drawing room.

Jane and Bob sat next to each other on one of the sofas in front of the fireplace and Amelia sat opposite while

Archie and Billy were standing at the fireside chatting, "do come and join us Inspector," said Jane as she gestured for them to join her on the sofas.

The Inspector immediately dashed over to sit next to Amelia and Sergeant Collins sat next to him leaving James who came in last to sit next to Bob, who stood up and was about to speak when the French doors opened and a rather dishevelled man burst in brandishing a single barrelled shotgun.

"Nobody move," he shouted, "I want you all to stay exactly where you are, where I can see you, if any of you try anything, I'll let you have it, I'm not messing about you know."

Bob stood up slowly and said, "look here old man, I don't know who you are or what you want but you do realise if you use that thing and kill one of us, you'll hang for murder."

James stood up slowly and said, "you can sit down Bob, I know exactly who this fellow is and why he's here," said James, and turning to the man, "shall I tell them or will you?"

"Go on then, if you're so damn clever," replied the man.

"Certainly," said James, "this is Major Trevor Lawrence and for the benefit of those of you who have never seen this man before I can tell you, Major Lawrence was mentioned in Dispatches for his gallant or meritorious actions during The Battle of the Somme in August 1916, I found details of his actions when I was going through Amelia's research."

"It appears that the good Major here and a Corporal were advancing towards the German lines and had got as far as the enemy trenches where they bravely fought off six German soldiers and the Corporal was shot in the head and the Major bayonetted in the leg."

"The Major then singlehandedly dragged the Corporal back to their own lines where they were taken to the Hospital unit and treated for their wounds, unfortunately the Corporal died before regaining consciousness, the Major later received a medal, the Distinguished Service Order and after the war went back to his Estate in Devon."

"Well, that's a very interesting story James," said Bob, "but I still have no idea why this man is standing in my drawing room pointing a loaded shotgun at us."

"The only reason I came across this information," said James, "was the fact that it confirmed the death of the Corporal whose name was Henry Eddleton, you may also be aware of his illustrious predecessor and former owner of Brightmoor, Lord Eddleton."

"I'm still, none the wiser as to why this fellow is here," said Bob who was by now getting rather agitated.

"I'm sorry," said James, "I think I can help to clarify the

situation for you," he paused, "the story of the Major and the Corporal is true in most respects except; I believe the two soldiers fell together into a shell hole but it was the Major and not the Corporal who had received the head wound and was unconscious when the Corporal swapped tags and uniforms and taking his bayonet he stabbed himself in the thigh and having dragged him back to the hospital the Major now dressed as the Corporal died, Henry Eddleton was then able to take on the identity of Major Trevor Lawrence."

The intruder, now identified as Henry Eddleton then said, "oh yes, very clever but I'm still the one here holding the gun, I'll tell you something about being the Major Lawrence, it proved to me where I belonged, I should be the one with all this, the money, the house."

"I thought you had the Majors estate," said Bob.

"That didn't last, I was swindled out of it by unscrupulous bookies," said Henry, "and now I expect you to help me get back on my feet, as I said before, give me my share, or you will die."

Archie was thinking of making a dash for it and tackling the intruder but thought better of it as he tripped on the corner of the fireplace and grabbed the bell to steady himself.

"Don't you try it," shouted Henry, "or someone will die here tonight, I mean it."

"I believe someone has already died," said James, "what about farmer Smith."

"He was collateral damage," said Henry, "it's what happens in war."

"This isn't war though, is it?" said James.

"The poor fellow was only killed because he took my hat by mistake," said Bob.

"It wasn't my fault," said Henry agitatedly, "he shouldn't have been wearing your hat."

Bob thought he would try to defuse the situation and said, "perhaps we can help you but I can't do anything tonight you'll have to wait a day or so."

This seemed to calm Henry down momentarily, when suddenly the door behind him in the bookcase opened and Wilson the Butler stepped smartly into the room and clumped Henry round the back of the head with the heavy silver tray, he carried with him, causing Henry to crumble unconscious to the floor.

"Tickety-boo," he said.

James quickly stepped forward and unloaded the shotgun and Sergeant Collins handcuffed Henry and dragged him off to the waiting Police car outside.

"Well, aren't we doing well today Inspector, first a jewel thief and now a murderer," said James, "that's another feather for your cap."

"Once again I am indebted to you Sir," said the Inspector.

"And so am I," said Bob, "Thank you, James and Archie, bravo to the Arbuthnott and Cluff Detective Agency for a job well done, I think that calls for Champagne, if you wouldn't mind Wilson.

"Certainly Sir," said Wilson, "Tickety-boo Sir, Tickety-boo."

ABOUT THE AUTHOR

Joe Wells has written eight children's books and a book of plays, one of which, Dulce Et Decorum Est Pro Patria Mori, was produced for the radio. He has another play which tells the story of a friendly fire incident on day three of World War Two, called The Battle of Barking Creek.